A FOOLISH VIRGIN

Ida Simons

A FOOLISH VIRGIN

Translated from the Dutch by
Liz Waters

MACLEHOSE PRESS
QUERCUS · LONDON

First published in the Dutch language as *Een dwaze maagd* in 1959 by
A. A. M. Stols, 's-Gravenhage
Reissued in 2014 by Uitgeverij Cossée, Amsterdam
First published in Great Britain in 2016

This paperback edition first published in 2017 by

MacLehose Press
An imprint of Quercus Publishing Ltd
Carmelite House
50 Victoria Embankment
London EC4Y 0DZ

AN HACHETTE UK COMPANY

This book was published with the support of
the Dutch Foundation for Literature

N ederlands
letterenfonds
dutch foundation
for literature

ISBN (MMP) 978 0 85705 406 7

10 9 8 7 6 5 4 3 2 1

Designed and typeset in Haarlemmer by Libanus Press, Marlborough
Printed and bound in Great Britain by Clays Ltd, St Ives plc

For Corry Le Poole-Bauer

CONTENTS

FROM MY MOTHER'S LIBRARY

by

Eva Cossée

My mother had to break off her studies during the German occupation of the Netherlands because she refused to sign her certificate of Aryan identity. She met my father through her church and supported him in his resistance activities. After the war she looked after their three children and continued her education, worked as a teacher, learned seven languages and read (almost) everything – preferably books of opinionated and independent women.

Ida Simons was a similar kind of woman. My mother gave me her novel, *A Foolish Virgin*, when I was fourteen or fifteen, and at the time I thought: she's trying to encourage me to play the piano, to play like Gittel in the book, with passion and commitment.

Many years later, after my mother's death and as I was clearing out my parents' house, I came upon the novel again; it was where on her bookshelves it always had been. I took it away with me, and when I reread it I immediately understood why my mother had so recommended it to me at the time. As a young girl I must have been just as guileless and dewy-eyed as Gittel. In *A Foolish Virgin* Ida Simons describes convincingly the consequences of gullibility, and that even in the circle of one's own family, it is sensible to make certain distinctions: who can you trust and who not; in whom can you have infinite confidence, or not; with whom can you discuss your hopes for life and for your future, and with whom should you rather not?

On my second reading I understood from the very first page why it had become a bestseller so soon after it was first published in 1959, and set on a level by critics with the work of Harry Mulisch and other literary luminaries. The musical tone, the stylistic fluency, the wit and the vivid portrait of a colourful Jewish community in the 1920s, now irrevocably a thing of the past, capture the reader's attention from the very first page and hold it to the end.

Ida Simons was born Ida Rosenheimer in Antwerp, Belgium, in 1911, eight years before my mother. At home the Rosenheimers spoke German, English and Yiddish. With the outbreak of the First World War, the Rosenheimers moved to the Belgisch Park district of Scheveningen (The Hague), became Dutch nationals and lived very close to my parents. Ida Simons stayed there until her death. She married David Simons, a lawyer, and soon made a career for herself as an internationally celebrated concert pianist.

In 1941 the German occupying forces forbad Jewish artists from performing in public. Thereafter Ida Simons was only able to play in her home, or at the homes of friends. Since my parents hosted clandestine house concerts so that the artists could continue to earn a little money, it is conceivable that Ida Simons may have sat at our grand piano at home. Sadly there is no-one still alive who is able to confirm this.

The Simons were deported to Westerbork transit camp in 1943. The camp was a large and efficient industry, with agriculture and gardens, a laundry, post office, hospital, workshops, kitchens and warehouses. It also had a choir, an orchestra and a cabaret. There Ida Simons took part in chamber concerts, playing pieces by Felix Mendelssohn-Bartholdy and Gustav Mahler, among others.

One year later, Ida and David Simons, together with their son Jan, were brought to Theresienstadt on the penultimate transport, and on 5th February, 1945, they were told to prepare themselves for a long journey. They were transported in a normal passenger train to the Swiss border, through a

Germany bombed to ruins. The travellers were told to remove the Stars of David from their clothing, the men were given shaving kits, and the women were told to doll themselves up with ersatz make-up. Ida Simons called it "the great miracle". Today we know that this was a one-off action by Himmler, in which Jews were exchanged for munitions. When Hitler learned of it, he forbad any further such exchanges.

After the war Ida Simons endeavoured to continue with her musical career. But her time in the camps had damaged her health to the extent that she had to give up her profession after a tour across America. Back in Scheveningen she began to write, and she published a volume of poetry as well as several short stories. In 1959 she became a famous novelist overnight with the publication of *A Foolish Virgin*. The book was universally praised in reviews and chosen as one of three "Best Books of the Year". Simons was already working on the sequel, a novel about Gittel as a grown woman, when she died suddenly and unexpectedly in 1960. That novel, *Like Water in the Desert*, was published posthumously and also found its way onto my mother's bookshelves.

A Foolish Virgin (*Een dwaze maagd*) was reissued in the Netherlands in 2014, fifty-five years after its first publication, and once again found enthusiastic readers who embraced the author above all for her individual tone and her subtle humour. The novel has now been translated into twenty-two languages. My mother, who was also a teacher of religion, may have detected – with a wink – some celestial determination in all this. But for me the novel represents a very special legacy. It is a sadness that neither Ida Simons nor my mother were able to enjoy the international success of *A Foolish Virgin*.

Eva Cossée is the Dutch publisher at Uitgeverij Cossée of notable authors such as J. M. Coetzee, David Grossman, Gerbrand Bakker, Zeruya Shalev, Bernhard Schlink and Hans Fallada.

"Anyone is capable of restraining a desperate person at the last minute. You need to give them a cup of coffee or a strong drink at a suitable moment or tell them they'll look unappetising or stupid as a corpse. The main thing is not to shirk that small duty; you have to have the coffee or the drink ready in your heart, as it were."

Marnix Gijsen, *The Man of the Day after Tomorrow*

I

FROM A YOUNG AGE I WAS USED TO HEARING MY FATHER
say, almost daily, that he had done his fellow man a serious
disservice by not becoming a funeral director. He was firmly
convinced that from that moment the population of our
planet would have consisted exclusively of immortals.

He was a *schlemiel* and he knew it; he told more than
one sour joke on the subject. On weekdays there was little
harm in them, but on festival days a simple remark like the
one about the funeral business was sufficient to spark a fierce
quarrel.

On Sundays and holidays my parents fought like cat
and dog.

Although they got along reasonably well otherwise, it all
added up, because the Jews are lumbered with a double set of
feast days. It was therefore a point of great importance for me
to know as early as possible on which dates our own were to

fall in the coming year. Once I had learned to read, I took to looking them up ahead of time, in December, the moment the new calendar came out.

With alarming frequency our feast days fell immediately before or after those celebrated by the remainder of humanity and in advance they dropped like stones around my heart, since with my father in the house for four days in a row it was inevitable that the conversation would turn to Uncle Salomon and Captain Frans Banning Cocq.

Whatever might have given rise to disputes between my parents and whatever the outcome of their disagreements, there was always a point at which they were both of the same mind to the extent that, in unison, they cursed Uncle Salomon and the famous captain from the bottom of their hearts.

When this occurred with more than the usual vehemence, my mother would take me back with her to her parental home. Until I met the Mardells in my native city, I thought the trip a very meagre pleasure; after I met them the weekly battle between my parents acquired the thrilling character of a game of chance. If it developed into a major quarrel, with no prospect of speedy reconciliation, the prize was mine: Antwerp. But as with any lottery, there were more tickets than prizes. Usually the row fizzled out and I could only hope for better luck on a future feast day.

Before Uncle Salomon and the captain intervened with such disastrous effect, my father had experienced several happy years in Antwerp. He spoke of it as a lost paradise, where he occupied himself entirely with horse riding, fencing and visits to the opera. Those fond memories did not quite chime with reality. For a start, he was forced to spend ten hours a day engaged in work for which he lacked any inclination or aptitude. He would have liked to become a violinist, but his parents regarded a musician's life as insufficiently exalted for a son of their family, which considered itself distinguished. Instead he had to go into trade and was apprenticed to manufacturers with whom they were on friendly terms. His total unsuitability for business life did not come to light there, unless perhaps it was concealed out of politeness towards his parents. He never mentioned how he came to be living in Antwerp, although he did tell us it was love at first sight and that he decided there and then to stay. He participated in all the city had to offer by way of enjoyable recreation, but unfortunately he was a serious, responsible young man who shunned frivolous pleasures, and for that omission he was punished with great severity.

Every day he ate a hot meal with a young compatriot in the only eating place that provided food prepared according to the Jewish dietary laws. The owner knew the power of his kosher monopoly – the diners had no say at all. Seated at one of four round tables in a small, shadowy room, they meekly ate whatever was served up to them.

One spring afternoon, half a century ago, a colourful group appeared in those sombre surroundings: three girls and three boys, accompanied by their parents and a small, strikingly blonde woman. According to my father it was as if a flock of humming birds had by accident found themselves in a sparrow colony. They all chirruped and twittered at once in English, Dutch and Spanish, paying no heed to the commotion they were causing.

It was a black day for the owner of the restaurant. To the delight of his regular victims, the head of this outlandish family asked him where he had found the nerve to give such an ape pen the grand title of restaurant. "On the other hand," he continued charitably, "perhaps your food is excellent; it wouldn't be the first time I've been served a first-rate meal in a miserable hole."

The three girls wore white frocks and large straw hats extravagantly decorated with roses. Fresh in from Argentina the previous day, they had not yet found time to purchase clothes better suited to the cool western beaches. They were gratified to note that despite their silly headgear they were making a deep impression on guests at the other tables.

They must have been very pretty, those three sisters. Many have told me since, with a sigh, of their beauty.

"They had dark curly hair, velvety brown eyes, skin the colour of ancient ivory, small coral-red mouths with no need of lipstick . . ." Their former admirers always ended their accounts by commiserating with me for looking like my father.

Within five minutes he was determined either to marry the oldest girl or to die. While the other regulars were enjoying the terse style in which her father made known his displeasure at the grubby state of the tablecloth and the contemptible quality of the fare, that smitten idiot had already turned his thoughts to the furnishing of a house for her. He was too shy to venture a step in her direction and when he was removed from the premises with some force by his friend because they both needed to get back to work, he still did not know what his beloved was called, nor where she was living, nor whether he would ever have a chance to see her again.

He spent all his free time standing guard at the door to the restaurant, until the chef took pity on him and said he could save himself the trouble, since the proprietor and the father of the family had parted sworn enemies. On paying the bill the paterfamilias had remarked, "I've been here twice, the first time and the last." In response the proprietor forbad him entry to his establishment for ever and a day.

A week later my father met the hummingbirds in the

house of his employer, whom he visited every month in an official capacity. Had he been capable then of rational thought, he would have foreseen such a possibility; in the state he was in he regarded it as a miracle. A year of abject slavery began. Every week he asked the girl to marry him and every time she turned him down. He was teased without mercy by her brothers and sisters. Her mother used him as a messenger boy, and he was obliged to take her father on at chess or draughts and somehow to play in such a way that he lost every game, since the old man could not stand losing. The only person with any apparent sympathy for the fate of the unfortunate suitor was a small blonde woman whom he vaguely remembered from that fateful first encounter. She was called Rosalba and she ran the household. It was she who after a year told him he must go away because he stood no chance. He realised she had his best interests at heart and promised to leave as soon as he could.

He handed in his notice to his employer, wrote the girl a farewell letter, sent her and each of the other members of the household a keepsake, and prepared himself for travel.

A few days before he was due to return to his native country, he received a visit from the girl's father, who found him, pale and wretched, in bed. It was obvious he had barely eaten or slept in recent weeks. The elderly gentleman said he would miss his chess partner and did not want to allow him to leave before he had, in person, wished him *bon voyage* and much happiness in his future life. After a few reciprocal courtesies, the conversation faltered. Then the visitor noticed a postcard of "The Night Watch" on the bedside table.

"From my brother," the sorrowful lover said with a sigh. "You're welcome to read it." Uncle Salomon was notorious in the family for writing too much, too often, and too didactically. This time, in his small and ornate handwriting, he gave an exhaustive account of the "overwhelming" impression made by his first encounter with the "divine" painting: "Note above all the splendid depiction of the shadow cast by Captain Frans Banning Cocq's hand on the gold-coloured tunic worn by Willem van Ruytenburch, Lord of Vlaardingen! Greetings. Salomon."

The girl's father, surprised and touched that a young man could be so foolish as to write to his brother on such a subject, worked himself up on his way home into one of his celebrated rages, of which he was proud because they were a family trait.

At home he called his daughter to him. He slammed his fist on the table and told her she was to marry the young man she had so stubbornly rejected and that was that. The fact that the Century of the Child had already dawned did not trouble the elderly despot, in fact he refused, to his last breath, to acknowledge its reality.

He threatened her, using all the weapons that loving fathers in those days had no hesitation in deploying. The girl resisted, but to no avail.

A week later the engagement was celebrated and soon afterwards the marriage, which will not have been any unhappier than most.

A few years after I was born, the First World War broke out and our whole family fled en bloc to the Netherlands. After the war everyone could go home, apart from us. I discovered only then that my best friend Mili and her parents, Uncle Wally and Aunt Eva, were not members of our family. They had always lived in the coastal resort of Scheveningen, which looked deserted now that all the refugees had returned to their own hearths. Except for us, that is, since it had never occurred to my German father, who had lived in Belgium for far longer and cared far more about that country than the rest of the family, to have himself naturalised, although I understood this only much later. I took a while to get used to the idea that Mili was not my cousin, but it was certainly a relief to discover that I did not share her grandfather. I was afraid of him, even though he looked exactly like Puss in Boots; he was tiny in stature and wore a Kaiser Wilhelm moustache. How he came to have that moustache was a mystery, since one had only to mention the name of the failed emperor in his presence to make Grandpa Harry foam at the mouth with rage.

"It's because of the marks," Mili said, as if she were talking about a particularly nasty strain of measles.

Mili's parents moved to The Hague and persuaded mine to do likewise. My father failed to find work and began to engage in business on his own account. Expecting little to come of it, he rented a cheap upstairs apartment in one of the busiest and ugliest streets of the city.

Our collie could not adjust to city life. As soon as the front door was opened he threw himself, out of pure misery, into the midst of the traffic. After he had been run over several times my parents decided to sell him. "It's for his own good," they said. "You surely don't want him to be run down and killed by the tram, which is bound to happen if we keep him." He was bought and collected by someone who lived in Rijswijk, but the next day he was back, with a length of chewed rope on his collar. His new owner came to fetch him and led him away on a strong steel chain. After that second parting, which was far harder to bear than the first, I took an unreasonable dislike to the city. At school I was at first teased by my fellow pupils and later ignored, which made life nice and quiet.

Mili, two classes below me, was in a very different position. She always came out of school surrounded by a swarm of little girls, full of lively stories about all her pleasant experiences. She might perhaps have ended our friendship around then had we not been Mrs Antonius and Mrs Nielsen.

Mrs Antonius – Mili – was grand. She had a nice daughter, Louise, and a nice husband who was a government minister by profession. My husband, Nils Nielsen, was a Swedish painter. He owed both his nationality and his name to my profound admiration for *Nils Holgersson's Wonderful Journey across Sweden*.

We had a young son, Benjamino, Satan in child form. The game consisted of continually thinking up new ways of stressing the respectable character of everything that happened at the Antoniuses' house and what a mess it was at ours. My Nils did little apart from smearing himself and all the furnishings with paint immediately prior to a visit by the minister, who then shook his dignified head in disapproval. The men did not like each other, and sweet little Louise was terrified of Benjamino, so the women were continually having to soothe and apologise. We kept up this tedious little game for a very long time, on the way to school and on the way home. Elsewhere we were silent as the grave on the subject of our families.

Mili had corn-blonde curls and big light-blue eyes, as did her dream daughter Louise, but she was no cutie; she was wise for her years at all ages. Her parents soon understood they had a rare creature under their wing. Even when she was very young they allowed her to decide on many things that concerned her, with excellent results. In appearance Mili bore no resemblance to them. They both had dark hair and dark-brown eyes. Aunt Eva was a beautiful woman, but what I found most attractive of all about her was her speaking voice, which had the sweet murmuring sound of a pleasant, slow-running stream. She aspired only to the goal of making herself and others as cosy as possible. To achieve it she even overcame her innate laziness. Everywhere were vases of flowers, which she arranged herself, with great care and taste. She made the most delicious sweets and biscuits, and all the taps in the house were decorated by her with ribbons – the ones in the lavatories were of pink-and-white striped satin. Mili's father was an angular, lean man with bright eyes and a broad mouth. Bushy eyebrows grew over the top of his large hooked nose. Despite his appearance, he was convinced he was irresistible, and with good reason, since in his dealings with people he managed to give them a sense that they were both important and lovable. He was never distant or indifferent like other grownups when Mili and I entrusted our little worries to him, and he played cards and bingo with us as if his life depended on it. Whenever something either delighted or antagonised him, he would enrich our language with a new word that we, without further clarification, were expected to decipher and comprehend.

One Sunday afternoon, when Salomon and his accomplice had been called to mind yet again in bitter exchanges, my mother took me with her to Aunt Eva, someone she could always turn to when she needed to pour out her heart. Mili and I were sent upstairs so that our mothers could talk and cry undisturbed. Allowed down an hour later, we found them sitting in a state of deep contentment, with tear-stained faces, drinking tea. Uncle Wally, a passionate angler, went out every Sunday morning at sunrise. We heard him arrive home whistling and go upstairs to change into a different suit. A short time later he strode into the room in high spirits.

"So, tenderlies," he greeted us. "I'm ready for some tea."

Mili asked him if he had had a pleasant day.

"It was smooderly," he said. "In a word: smooderly. Everything went my way."

Mili and I congratulated him. He went to sit in his armchair, lit a cigarette, and then noticed the teary faces of his wife and her friend. He asked in dismay why they were sitting there like a pair of poophadonoes. Aunt Eva told him my mother was leaving for Antwerp the next day, taking me with her, and there was a chance we would never come back, because my mother was seriously contemplating a divorce and she had decided in any case to stay away for six months.

Wally was furious. "What a rot-apotheosis," he said. "This is clearly a case on the subject of which Wally will have to send himself a document."

Mili reddened to the depths of her throat and Aunt Eva turned pale. "Oh, please don't, Papa," Mili cajoled and Aunt Eva too urged him to forgo his intention this time, but even the pleas of that lovable voice could not make him change his mind.

He commanded Mili, in stern tones that admitted of no denial, to fetch paper and stamps from his room. "You know where everything is kept and I expect you straight back here, without chicanery or any fake hadderissio."

"Yes, Papa," Mili said, docile and dejected as I had never seen her before. I went upstairs with her and asked her to tell me what was about to happen, but she refused.

"You'll see," she said. "It's terrible. He's forever doing this. It sometimes drives Mama and me round the bend and it always proves him right, too."

With a deep sigh she laid the writing materials on the table in front of her father. He sat down, took a sheet of paper and, dictating to himself in a loud voice, began to write.

Document.
I, wise Wally, hereby declare in the presence of Thea, Eva, Gittel and Mili, in writing, verbally and solemnly,

the following: Thea asserts that she will opt for domicile with her family for six months or longer.

I, the aforementioned wise Wally, declare that before six weeks have passed she will have returned to her own address, and a good thing too!

Duly signed,
Wally.

This document will be opened in six weeks from the above date in the presence of the selfsame witnesses and Wally will be universally, humbly and officially recognised as having been right.

Duly signed,
Wally

The four witnesses looked and listened as if struck dumb; Uncle Wally folded the document into an envelope, sealed and stamped it, and wrote his office address on the front. Then Mili and I had to walk with him to the post box, so that, as he explained, we would later be able to declare under oath that the document really had been posted on that particular day, just in case new material should come to light in the meantime. As soon as Mili and I were up in her room again, she made me swear, in the name of our longstanding friendship, not to tell anyone about her father's wretched custom.

I said she could count on me, and that there were certain matters in my life too that I would not wish to see made public. That seemed to reassure her no end and she asked whether I found going to Antwerp again a pleasant prospect. "Perfectly horrible," I said. We had been there little more than a month earlier and after a trip like that I had to work myself to death at school to catch up with the lessons I had missed.

2

THERE WAS NO-ONE ON THE PLATFORM TO MEET US
and my mother said she had known in advance that it was
going to be a no-day. On a no-day everything went wrong
and yes-days were rare indeed.

We lugged our suitcases to the entrance and in time with
our footsteps my mother recited in sombre tones:

> Hark! Hark!
> The dogs do bark!
> The beggars are coming to town . . .
> Some in rags,
> And some in tags
> And one in a silken gown.

She knew I hated that rhyme, and she would not have tormented me with it so often *if she had seen the snow-lined*

street with tall yellow houses on either side, their pointed roofs piercing a low-hanging blanket of cloud that was painted red and purple by the setting sun.

Every house had a front garden, a square of gravel with at its centre a uniform bed of pink geraniums.

The residents had been warned to expect the beggars and had lowered the roll-down blinds in front of all the windows, but their fear seeped out through the cracks into the front gardens where their dogs stood guard, bouviers and sheepdogs and those big white ones that look as if they have been spattered with ink by an angry giant's hand. Now and then one of the dogs howled, having heard the beggars coming from far off, long before the street filled with furious shouts and the shuffling sound of worn-out feet. Hundreds they were: some hobbled along on crutches or dragged a wooden leg, others wore a black patch over an empty eye socket. They shouted that they were hungry and shook their fists at the yellow houses, but whenever they dared to mount the pavement the dogs growled and barked, opening their slavering mouths wide to show their teeth. Helpless and trapped in hunger and rags, the beggars were forced to move on. They jeered and roared, but they could not chase off the dogs.

Then the beggar in the silken gown walked by. Apricot-coloured silk it was, no less torn and tattered than the drab rags of the others and far less warm, but it gleamed in the rays of the setting sun and its sheen was intolerable to those walking closest

*to the beggar in the silken gown which made their own rags seem
even more shabby and soiled.*

*Hairy claws first expanded the holes in the rotting silk and
then tore open the pale skin underneath. When the man who had
worn the silken gown lay naked and still in the snow, the others
walked on past, calm, almost happy. Last to leave the street were
the beggars who had most difficulty walking. They took pleasure
in hitting the motionless form with their crutches.*

*When silence falls once more in the street, the dogs come out
of the gates …*

My mother and I told each other that perhaps someone
would be waiting for us outside, but we knew better. The
only way Grandmother could let us know she was less than
pleased by our visit was by failing to send anyone to fetch
us, since she had made it impossible for herself to say it outright.

Apart from my uncles Charlie and Fredie, all her children
were married, and it would have been far more sensible and
economical for her to move into a smaller home, but she
liked the big house on one of the broadest avenues of the city
and she resisted tooth and nail. "I continue to live in this
uncomfortable great barn of a house only so that all my
children and grandchildren can come home whenever they
feel like it," she said. She had thereby committed herself.
When my mother announced our visit she had to welcome us

even if her welcome was in no way sincere. That the house was difficult to live in, with all those long staircases and a kitchen in the basement, did not matter in the least to her. She had Rosalba to do all the work.

We were forced to take a taxi, since we had far more luggage with us than usual. After all, this time we were to be gone for six months.

When the driver stopped outside the house my mother groaned: "And now this!" Near the front door, Rosalba stood talking with Grandma Hofer. The driver unloaded our suitcases and to our relief Rosalba rummaged in the pocket of her apron and paid him. She seemed shorter and slighter than ever next to Grandma Hofer, a formidable woman who in her posture and clothing bore a strong resemblance to an expensive funeral coachman. In our family it was said that her tongue was made of sandpaper.

Rosalba kissed us and Grandma Hofer said, "Well, well, those two are here again; I thought you'd only just gone home." My mother asked, with respect, how the families of her two sisters were doing, both of whom were Grandma Hofer's daughters-in-law. "Lots of commotion, thank goodness," Grandma Hofer answered. "So everyone must be healthy."

She grabbed my chin, turned my face to the light and declared that I resembled my father as one drop of water resembles another. Rosalba said that in that case I looked like a very good man.

"Oh, what a good man," Grandma Hofer sneered. "Never eats glass, never drinks ink, and never overturns the tram. Poverty is no shame, but neither is it an honour." At that she gave Rosalba such a sound slap on the back that it almost knocked her over, then without deigning to say goodbye she marched off along the street like a grenadier.

How and where Rosalba came to be part of my mother's wild family no-one knows. For as long as she lived each of us took her modest presence and caring ways as a matter of course. She was part of the inventory and that was that. She was Protestant and English. She never learned any other language and how she managed to make herself understood in the far-off country to which she had followed my grandmother to keep house for her is one of the many mysteries surrounding her diminutive person. She never said a word about her own faith and no longer attended church. She guarded our spiritual well-being rigorously, however. In no kitchen where a Jewish woman held sway will the dietary laws have been adhered to more meticulously than in the one where Rosalba cooked so superbly and so super-kosher.

Every day a comedy was performed with the purpose of making Rosalba believe we were unaware of her illiteracy. Giving an exaggerated wink to all others present, Grandmother would think up one new excuse after another to read aloud to her from the newspaper, and if at Christmas a letter arrived from England from her only brother, it would be answered by one of us because Rosalba happened to have broken her spectacles.

She was far from stupid, but none of us ever tried to teach her the art of reading. We sensed that my grandmother would not have encouraged it.

As we were going into the house, Rosalba told us that Grandmother and Grandma Hofer were on a war footing once more. The two engaged in grim battles for first place in the hearts of the half-dozen grandchildren in whom they had shares. Grandmother was sitting in her armchair by the window with her needlework. She was small and stout and always wore frocks of heavy black silk with frills of snow-white lace, like the outfits worn by the late Queen Victoria. She believed her life resembled in many respects the life of that English monarch. She liked to describe herself as the mother-in-law of Europe and she too had been widowed young. She bore her widowhood with courage, not to say cheerfulness. She had fierce dark eyes and the skin of her round face was as unwrinkled and downy as a young girl's, a fact of which she was proud and to which she liked to draw attention.

Rosalba brought coffee and cake and my mother

managed so adroitly to tear Grandma Hofer to shreds that our reluctant hostess forgot her vexation with regard to our visit.

That diversionary manoeuvre, suggested by Rosalba with some subtlety, was a magnificent success.

"How lovely it is that you are here again," Grandmother said, and then the latest items of family news were discussed at length.

"How are things now between Isi and Sonja?" my mother said, smiling.

"Just you go out and play in the garden," Rosalba said to me. That was what I always had to do when talk turned to the black sheep of the family, the husband of my youngest aunt. He did not take marital loyalty too seriously and when reproaches on the subject reached his ears he would answer, unperturbed: "Even if you own the most beautiful Rembrandt in the world you nevertheless sometimes want to look at a different painting." Or: "The fact that a man loves one woman doesn't mean he has to hate all the others." There is not a great deal even a troublesome busybody can say in response to that.

Resigned, I walked down the stairs to the basement and along the dark passageway that led to the garden, a paltry triangular patch of ground bounded by high walls on all sides. Not one ray of sunlight could find its way in, and whatever was planted there immediately died – save two indestructible holly bushes that had grown bigger and more prickly each time I saw them. My aunts' houses all had small gardens and Mili lived with her parents in an upstairs apartment just like ours. *So it was good that I had a garden behind my house on the island, where roses and forget-me-nots bloomed all year round. Before I went to live there I bought Rollo, the collie, back from his new owner and every morning I took a walk along the beach with him. Apart from Blimbo and Juana, the Negro couple who took care of the house and garden, we were the island's only inhabitants. Mili was sometimes allowed to come and stay. My parents were too, but not both together, because I did not want to hear that whining about Banning Cocq on the island. Fritz Kreisler* and his accompanist were very welcome once a year and apart from that no-one was admitted unless specifically invited. Blimbo sat high up in the lighthouse and informed me from there of the appearance of any brazen miscreants trying to force their way in. Occasionally, if the weather was very fine, I visited Blimbo in his octagonal tower. A broad, white half-moon would appear on his dark face as he smiled and lent me his binoculars. I could very clearly make out the city on the mainland and the mountains beyond it, but it was rare for me to go there, I was far too happy on the island. Before leaving the turret*

---

* Fritz Kreisler (1875–1962), an Austrian-born violinist and composer.

room I always glanced at the corner where the round, green stones lay, to check that Blimbo was keeping up the supply. Rollo ran a long way ahead of me on the beach every time, but he always came back, with short barks, to have his head stroked. I started to feel hungry and told him we must get back home. The sea looked inviting; it was a little too early in the year for a swim, but perhaps I might chance it in the afternoon.

We had barely got indoors when the telephone rang. It could only be Blimbo and that meant trouble.

"What is it, Blimbo?"

"The boat from the mainland is in the harbour, Missy. Not expecting visitors today, are you?"

"No, Blimbo. Perhaps it's a parcel."

"I don't think so, Missy. Pedro, who usually brings the post, is not on the boat and only one lady has disembarked."

"Ask what her name is and what she wants."

I had to wait at the telephone for a moment. I could hear Blimbo's soft voice in the distance. He picked up the receiver again. "Are you still there, Missy?"

"Yes, of course, Blimbo. Who is the uninvited guest?"

"She says she's Grandma Hofer, that you know her well, and that she wishes to visit you."

"Stone, Blimbo."

Blimbo's aim was true, which was why I had hired him.

*

Uncle Isi must have had plenty to answer for, because I was not called upstairs again. After half an hour it grew too cold in the garden and I went to see the two maids, who were polishing brass with a deafening song. I bellowed the choruses along with them at the top of my voice. There was something in the atmosphere of that house that worked on the noise instincts. My uncles each had a gramophone and would compete at full volume, and any children who visited would start crying right at the front door. The radio had not yet begun its civilising work. If it had, the din would have been intolerable.

One of the ordeals of our stay was that I was expected to enjoy occupying myself with my far younger cousins on afternoons when the nannies had time off. My aunts entrusted their offspring to me while the nannies went to the cinema and expressed, in all insincerity, the hope that we would have a lovely time playing together. Blimbo was busy on days like that, because for me the game consisted of ensuring that the toddlers did not fall down the stairs. Rosalba quite understandably hid in her room until teatime.

I endured another ordeal every Friday evening. The uncles would bring a *shnorrer*, a beggar, with them from the synagogue, and he was always given a seat at the table between me and Rosalba. I suffered the chomping and slurping in silence, because although the *shnorrers'* table manners were primitive, I knew my grandmother would give me a thorough dressing down if I were to complain. During the week we often had our own "greener". The greeners were not *shnorrers*, they were young men from Poland or such parts who had moved to Antwerp to learn the diamond-cutter's trade. Once they had mastered it and begun to earn some money, they no longer wished to qualify for free meals, so a newly arrived greener would take the place of the previous one. Their honesty and solidarity were exemplary in that respect. They were quiet, shy boys, who spoke nothing but Polish and a type of Yiddish unintelligible to us. They gobbled down all they could and disappeared as soon as the meal was over, with a brief wave, as silent and shy as when they came in. Among the professional *shnorrers* were some colourful characters, since any *shnorrer* serious about his vocation was convinced he was fulfilling an important social function, one that was pleasing to the Lord. "Was he not placing his fellow man in a position to exercise charity that would be noted, to the credit of the benefactor, by the angel appointed for that purpose?"

"Was that not of far greater value than a few mouthfuls of food or a handful of coins?"

"Who, therefore, was in fact the true benefactor?"

The high-flown notion they entertained of their task made associating with the *shnorrers* easy, and free of the simulated humility and gratitude that often mar the beggar–philanthropist relationship.

The professional *shnorrer* would usually carry a letter in Hebrew – counterfeit or otherwise – from a rabbi seeking support for a needy community or *yeshiva* in Poland. He would go with it to a colleague already settled in Antwerp who, for a percentage, provided him with a list of the better-off members of the Jewish community. Only the *shnorrers* knew where to find such well-informed "Antwerpians". Many stories about them were doing the rounds, all very similar. Every charitable family had its own version concerning the chutzpah of the *shnorrer* and the good humour with which it was met. On one occasion I had the privilege of encountering a master of the art.

He strolled in early on a wintry Friday afternoon. He was wearing a long caftan of black silk and an expensive fur hat, pressed down over his red hair at a rakish angle. A narrow, prickly beard framed his broad, flushed face. He was merriment personified and he amused us by singing songs for an hour. First he told us the gist of each song, because we could not understand his Yiddish too well; he spoke very good German. After a while he looked at the clock.

"Four o'clock," he said. "Before we go to *shul* I have just enough time to deal with a client."

He pulled the famous list from his pocket.

"Pick one for me, one who doesn't live too far away," he said with a jovial smile to Charlie, who had just come in. "And then take me there." Charlie told us later that the rogue had walked along the street beside him singing loudly and bought a fat cigar, which he lit and smoked with obvious enjoyment. Charlie judged it necessary to point out to him that this way of behaving would not make a good impression on the client from whom he was hoping to extract funds.

"This whippersnapper is trying to teach me my job," the redhead laughed, and Charlie swore to us that after the client's door opened, the *shnorrer* crossed the threshold chalk white and sobbing, noisily and compellingly bewailing his fate.

He returned to us even more cheerful, if possible, than he had left. To my grandmother's enquiry as to whether all had gone according to plan he answered, "I have no grounds for dissatisfaction."

At table he was the most agreeable guest, although the meal failed to win his unmitigated approval.

"Where is the fish?" he said, when the soup was followed by a meat course. Grandmother apologised by saying that the eating of fish on Friday evenings was not the custom among us in the Low Countries. "Never mind, that's fine," the *shnorrer* said, in the best of humour. "But you don't know what you are missing."

He told one joke after another and there was one that

I remembered, because nobody would explain to me what was so funny about it.

"One fine day," the red-haired *shnorrer* told us, "I arrived at a small town just in time for *Shabbat*. It was winter, a thick pelt of snow lay on the road and all the houses were wearing white skull-caps. With a little effort I found the way to *shul*. I was cold and hungry. After the service I asked the *shamus* whether he perhaps knew of a house where I could eat."

"'You're in luck,' the *shamus* says. 'You can eat at the rabbi's.'

"'The rabbi,' I said, startled, since we all know that our *rabbanim* (God shall keep them all healthy and to a hundred and twenty shall they live) are not well off. You won't be served a meal by them such as I've eaten here this evening (even if there wasn't any fish). The *shamus* understood. 'Our rabbi is a wealthy man,' he said. 'An excellent meal will be served to you. You will be more than satisfied.' And he told me where to go.

"I arrived at the house, a big white house, and knocked at the door. After a short time a woman answered. Oh, what a woman!" The redhead raised his hands and eyes to heaven.

"A beauty, an angel from paradise! I stammered my apologies, thinking I had knocked at the wrong door, but the beautiful woman gave me an amiable smile. Oh, what a smile!

It conjured dimples into her pink cheeks and revealed teeth like pearls.

"She invited me in and told me she was the *rebbetzin*.

"Our *rebbetzins* are good, honest women. Sometimes they can be very sensible, too. They have no need to be beautiful and therefore most of them aren't. (God bless them.) I'd never seen a *rebbetzin* like this one before.

"I walked behind her into the dining room, a large room with a richly laden table.

"There sat the rabbi, as grand as a king, in a chair like a throne with silken cushions. He greeted me, serious but friendly, and showed me where to sit. The beautiful woman lit the candles in the large shining candelabra and the light of the flames was reflected so softly in her big dark eyes that it silenced even me for a moment.

"She brought us the soup herself, in a silver dish. As is proper, she served her husband first. The rabbi tasted the soup, shook his head, picked up the salt cellar in one hand and the pepper pot in the other and sprinkled large quantities from each of them into his soup plate. Again horror clutched at my heart. 'She's far too beautiful to be a good cook,' I thought, and when she ladled out my soup I took only a little on my spoon and tasted . . . with great caution . . . It was an outstanding soup, a heavenly soup. I emptied my plate with relish and did not refuse when the *rebbetzin* offered to fill it again. She brought in the fish. Carp with raisins, my favourite dish. (A meal without carp and raisins is no meal at all, I always say.) Again the rabbi tasted, shook his head, and tossed handfuls of pepper and salt over that sublime carp. A pity and a shame it was. I could detect not a hint of surprise on the sweet, peaceful face across from me. It seemed to be a habit of the rabbi and he persisted in it up to and including the *kugel*. He scattered pepper and salt over that too.

"After the prayer of thanksgiving I could stand it no longer.

"'Rabbi,' I said to him, as he sat staring ahead, deep in thought. 'Rabbi, may I ask you something?'

"'Certainly my son,' he said. 'Ask what you have to ask.'

"'Rabbi,' I said. 'Rabbi, everything was so delicious this evening. Why did you spoil that exquisite food by scattering so much pepper and salt over it?'

"'I thought you might ask,' the rabbi sighed. 'They all ask me that. I'll try to explain. Listen. According to the books there must in all things here on earth remain something to be desired. I try to live by the teachings. When I am served food that is entirely to my taste, I find it necessary to add something that makes it rather less appetising to me, because nothing here on earth can be perfect. Can you understand that?'

"'Yes, rabbi,' I said. 'I understand it and I thank you for

your willingness to explain it to me with such clarity and may I ask you something else?'

"'Certainly,' said the rabbi. 'Just ask, my son.'

"'How much salt and pepper do you need to throw over your wife?'"

Although the joke went over my head, it amused me no end because our minstrel did such a good job of telling it. He could change the colour of his face at will. When he spoke in the voice of the rabbi he turned pale, his eyes took on a grave, contemplative expression, and even his hands seemed to grow longer and narrower. When he spoke as the *rebbetzin* we saw in him the enchanting young woman, despite his bristly chin-strap beard.

Before he left, my grandmother thanked him, on behalf of us all, for his pleasant company and his beautiful singing. A melancholy smile appeared on his face, which had now become earnest and ashen.

"I'm glad and thankful if I've entertained you with my songs and jokes and I'll tell you why. I am a poor sinner, who often strays from the right path. Sometimes, at night, when I cannot sleep (for I sleep in a different bed each night), I ask myself what will become of me and what awaits me after the Angel of Death has fetched me.

"I once spoke about this with a wise man.

"'Do not concern yourself,' he said. 'Things always turn out well for a musical fool such as you, in the future world as well as here. The righteous will need to make light of your many sins, out of self-interest, because it would be as unpleasant up there as it would be down here below without the singers, fools and poets.'"

3

LUCIE LATER SAID THAT SHE CAME TO THE SYNAGOGUE
that Saturday morning solely in order to meet me. She would
not have come otherwise and her unexpected presence caused
something of a stir, even though she went to sit quietly in the
back row of seats so as not to attract attention.

When I stayed with Grandmother I had to go to *shul* with
her every week. In those days Hebrew was not yet generally
taught as a living language, so although I had learned to read
it, I could not follow the service. I lost track straight away and
kept casting furtive glances at Grandmother; each time she
turned a page in her prayer book I did the same in mine. I would
never have dared to admit to anyone that I found the service
interminable, least of all to myself, because I was very pious.

The sexes sat apart at our service of worship, so we
climbed a long staircase to the women's section of the synagogue to take our seats behind a barrier intended to protect

us from any lustful looks cast by the men sitting below. When I recall the physical beauty on show in our section, it strikes me that even without a barrier we would not have been too much troubled by lustful looks.

After a while I needed to deploy all kinds of strategies to avoid falling asleep. First I tried to spot my uncles and other men I knew in the men's section, through the bars of the barrier. They were dressed in sober dark suits and had black-and-white prayer shawls around their shoulders. They wore skull-caps, or in some cases a kind of black felt Homburg that was later given the blessing and name of an English cabinet minister.

When I had finished examining the men, I started counting the squares in the grating that separated us from them and after that the number of women in the congregation wearing wigs. There were quite a few who wore the compulsory *sheitel* of the married Jewish woman under their pompous *Shabbat* hats. The one worn by my grandmother must have been a source of irritation to the other devout women, since she was clever enough to place piety at the service of vanity. She always had hers made in Paris by a famous wig artist, of silky, bronze-coloured hair full of curls and waves, decorated with gaily glistening combs and pins.

Under the low ceiling there was a smell of old women, lavender water and hunger, because the service had to be digested on an empty stomach. On this particular occasion the stuffy air made me even dizzier than usual because I had reached the age of twelve, when a Jewish woman is regarded as mature enough to participate in the duties imposed upon her by her faith, and Rosalba had for the first time withheld from me the "child's morsel".

"You're not allowed to have that anymore now," she said, always stricter about such compliance than Grandmother, who would have turned a blind eye to a few nibbles of ginger cake even had I been a fully grown woman. Despite the fear that Our Lord would strike me down with lightning if He noticed, I nodded off that morning. At the end of the service I was startled awake by the animated conversation of the other women, who were as pleased as I was at no longer having to sit still.

Grandma Hofer squeezed past us with a cool nod and the aunts came to fetch Grandmother to accompany her outside.

We all walked to Grandmother's house, where Rosalba had meanwhile prepared a substantial breakfast, but this time events took a different course from usual, because on the way out Miss Lucie Mardell came up to me, a fact that caused considerable consternation in the female ranks of my family. Miss Mardell was far grander than we were, which is to say than my mother's family was. My father's family belonged, by his account, to the most ancient aristocracy.

Ideas about social status were quite diverse in our community. Every clique had another to be scornful about. The Jews who had come from Germany enjoyed that pleasure with regard to the Poles, who felt themselves far superior to the "Ollanders", who in turn thought all the rest a worthless bunch, so everyone had reason to feel content. The "true Belgians", who had been living in the city for a generation or longer, did not think a single mortal from any other group worthy of so much as a glance, aside from a few "Fine People" who were honoured and esteemed by all no matter what their origin. How they had achieved that status was, in the main, impossible to comprehend, since it had nothing to do with learning or material well-being. Once they had managed to acquire such a designation, however, the fortunate few put on proud faces, on which insiders could read: "I'm acknowledged to be a 'Fine Person' and the usual prejudices do not apply to me."

Lucie's father was not by anyone's definition a "Fine Person". He was gruff and unapproachable. With the exception of my father, who in the golden age before his marriage had been a friend of Mr Mardell, none of my family had ever seen more of his house than the ground floor where he had his office. Lucie and her father were so grand that they associated with no-one at all in our community and now, to my astonishment, she spoke to me. "Are you the girl who can play the piano so beautifully?" she said, with a mocking smile in her big, light-grey eyes and on her narrow lips, a smile I would learn to love and fear. She was wearing a dark-green coat and perched on her light-brown hair was a small, grey fur hat. A snob like most children, I relished the barely disguised envy and curiosity of my grandmother and the aunts. Lucie put her hand on my shoulder and drove me before her out onto the street. It was plain that Grandmother was torn. Although flattered at the interest paid by the highest in the land, she was peeved that it applied to me alone.

"Listen," Lucie said. "With them" – she gave a haughty nod in the direction of my family – "do you have a good instrument?"

"Not terribly good," I said, which was true, because the entire family had learned to play on that poor little piano and it was therefore understandable that it had become chronically out of tune.

"I'll ask if you can come and play on ours; we have a very good Steinway," Lucie said. She was courteous and amiable towards everyone and in the blink of an eye she had obtained the necessary permission from my astonished grandmother.

"I don't want her walking the streets on her own," was her final, feeble attempt at resistance.

"I'll send my housekeeper, or come to fetch her myself," Lucie said. She nodded affably at the array of cross faces and to me she said, "I'll see you on Monday at ten!" On the way home, all the pent-up exasperation burst loose.

"What a nerve!"

"Who does she think she is?"

"You should never have agreed to it, Mother."

"Won't even look at the rest of us and then takes Gittel off to play the piano and Gittel doesn't even like the idea of going, do you child? To that tiresome person?"

"I don't care how tiresome she is, as long as there's a good grand piano," I said.

On Monday morning I was given an extra polishing and for the sake of the family honour a new white ribbon was tied in my hair. At the appointed hour Lucie came to fetch me. "I'll take good care of her." She smiled, sweet as anything, at Grandmother. But once we were out on the street she said, "Phew, I thought right at the last moment they were going to forbid you to come."

The Mardells' house, the most beautiful in the whole avenue, was diagonally across from my grandmother's, but to my surprise we did not go straight there. "We have to discuss the order of the ceremony," Lucie said with mock seriousness. "You'll find it annoying, I'm sure, but to start with you'll be introduced to everyone in the house; there's no escaping it on your first visit." She gave my ribbon a tug. "Just tell me honestly, you do find that annoying, don't you?"

I nodded and I believe it was then that I began to adore her.

"My father wants to see you because he knows your father well, but that won't take long, as he's always busy and he's taciturn by nature. You won't be rid of Bertha so quickly. Bertha is an old retainer, like Rosalba at your house." Lucie's mother had died young and Bertha regarded Lucie as her own child. "Which can sometimes be very irritating, because she keeps nagging me to get married and I haven't the slightest desire to do so." Next I would be introduced to Salvinia Natans, Menie Oberberg and Gabriel, all three of whom worked in the office of the bank. "Salvinia and Menie have just become engaged, thank God; we all had a hard time until then."

Salvinia and Menie had worked in the office for three years and were deeply in love all that time without daring to say a word about it. But Salvinia kept fainting and Menie grew so spectrally thin that it started to exasperate Lucie's father. He asked for her hand on Menie's behalf, without consulting him in advance, then conveyed to him her ecstatic "yes". Ever since that moment they had both been glowing with happiness.

"And Gabriel?"

"Oh, Gabriel is the youngest employee," Lucie said in a dismissive tone. "After you've done your duty and been properly introduced to everyone you'll first have to play something for me, then you'll get a cup of hot chocolate and I'll leave you alone, if that's what you'd like. Otherwise I'll stay with you and do some needlework. I can be very quiet." I knew from experience what so-called being quiet was like and I said with as much civility as I could muster that of course she need not absent herself on my account. Lucie, clever thing that she was, saw through me at once. "You don't believe it, eh?" She laughed. "That I can sit still. But you'll see."

Then we crossed the road and before long we were standing at the tall white door of the big house. A fat blonde woman in a white pinafore let us in, kissed me on both cheeks and began a long story about "your esteemed papa", whom she appeared to think very nice. Lucie gave me a wink and said, "Bertha, tell the rest another time. My father is waiting for us."

She knocked on a door that had an office hatch built into it and I walked behind her into a room where two men and a woman were labouring away with great diligence at, as far as I could tell, adding up. Salvinia, short, fat and dark, had spectacles and no neck. Her eyes fixed on Menie, she crouched down next to me and threw her arms around me. Menie was so moved by this show of motherliness that he had to wipe his spectacles and then his almost bald head. Salvinia said she hoped she would have six daughters and I had to endure a kiss from her too. After that I shook Menie's damp hand and only then did I get a good look at Gabriel – the Angel Gabriel in a threadbare black suit with oversleeves.

His dark-blue eyes smiled at me out of such an uncommonly captivating face that I stared at him with my mouth open. His copper-coloured hair gleamed as if a sun invisible to ordinary mortals was shining on him. One untidy lock fell across a high, white forehead onto one of his dark eyebrows. The ink stains on his fingers could not detract from the noble appearance of his long hands.

"Shall I tell Mr Mardell you're here, Miss Mardell? I believe he is free at the moment."

"Yes please, Gabriel." Lucie nodded, and only after he had left the room did I see how drab and unattractive it was with its unpainted woodwork and dark curtains. The only decoration was a large office calendar with all kinds of illegible scrawls all over it. Gabriel came back and held the door open for us. He was tall and slim, almost a head taller than Lucie, who at that time I thought too tall for a woman. "I can't just walk into my father's room," she explained to me in the corridor. "Often very important people come to talk to him." She knocked on a door that seemed to be made of congealed honey and after a welcoming voice called out "Come in" I saw Mr Mardell's room for the first time, finding it very strange because there was no furniture apart from a desk and three chairs. The walls were lined with bookshelves up to a third of their height, and above that they were covered in paintings. Behind the desk, which was made of the same strange wood as the door, sat Lucie's father, a tall, elegant man with light-brown hair, greying at the temples, and one of those neutral faces about which the *goyim* say that they do not look at all Jewish.

He stood up as we entered and said with gravity: "So, here we have the *artiste*, then. How is your father doing?"

He put that question to me every time I saw him. For him my mother and her family did not exist. I answered that my father was very well, thank you, and asked if I might be allowed to look at the paintings.

"Yes, please do, and afterwards you must tell me what you think of them."

Mr Mardell would always treat me as if I was well into my sixties.

Here none of the paintings were at all like those hanging on Grandmother's walls. I found them very odd, one in particular, which depicted a purple woman with a slapdash green belly. What most of the others were supposed to be I simply could not tell, which was less troubling. "Well," Mr Mardell said when I had looked at them all. "Let me hear your opinion."

"My father says that you know what is beautiful long before other people do," I said. "So these paintings are sure to become beautiful at some point."

"But right now you don't see that in them?" he said. No, I did not see that and I thought it lame to pretend that I did. "Isn't there a single canvas that meets with your approval?" I pointed to a painting of a low white house beside a wet ditch, surrounded by trees, painted on a misty afternoon in autumn. A single bright stroke of orange formed a shining trace of the route by which the sun had gone down. "That October house."

Lucie laughed: "Silly girl. Why October house?"

"It's October," I insisted. "You can smell that they've been burning leaves in the garden in the afternoon," and Mr Mardell asked why I found it beautiful.

"Because it's such a happy house that the people who live in it don't care if it's cold and dark outside," I stammered, very shy all of a sudden because Lucie thought me a silly girl.

"Go on," she said. "Upstairs. Otherwise you'll soon be saying it's my fault that you haven't had enough time to play." She gave me a wink and everything was right again between us. When I tried to take my leave of Mr Mardell he said he would like to listen for a while too. "If you don't have any objection, that is."

That first morning I saw nothing in the room we went

into apart from the Steinway. There are few pianos that have a soul and among the delightful exceptions was the Mardells' grand. Lucie's father did not stay with us for long. He said I could come and play whenever I liked, in the afternoons as well. The house had so many other rooms that I would not be in anyone's way.

Lucie kept her word. She was as quiet as a mouse, doing needlework so that I could enjoy playing undisturbed. At twelve o'clock she folded away her work and said she would take me home. "Do you think you'd like to come back tomorrow?" she said, teasing me. I failed to think of a witty answer.

At Grandmother's I was subjected to a veritable cross-examination, but I gave little away.

The following morning "the October house" was hanging next to the grand piano.

"My father says it can stay here for as long as you come to play," Lucie said. "That's a great honour. He's never lent me any of his paintings."

Within a week I was Lucie's slave.

If anyone had reminded me that when I first saw her I thought her a beanpole, I would have denied it indignantly. She told me straight away to call her by her first name and I rolled it over my tongue like a delicacy. For me an important part of the great charm she exuded lay in the fact that she was very different from all the women I knew. She said little, rarely smiled, and was a picture of self-assurance.

She wore clothes and colours that suited her, not just those that happened to be in fashion. In a time when the entirety of the female sex wore its hair cut short like a man's and shaved at the nape, hers was long, parted in the middle, with a soft little chignon at her neck. I felt glad that my mother had forbidden me to have mine cut off despite my pleading.

My hair was not dark blonde and wavy, however, but straight and black as soot. I asked my grandmother if she had ever heard of someone's hair changing colour from one day to the next. As far as she knew, she said, it had only ever happened to the Count of Monte Cristo after he spent a night in a cavern in the company of a number of corpses. I was not minded to try that.

The Mardells' house was solid and firm. The rattle of the typewriters played upon by Menie and Salvinia did not penetrate to the room where the grand piano stood. It always took me quite an effort to avoid that pair of lovers on my way upstairs, since they so enjoyed showing each other how affectionate they could be towards children. There was no escaping Bertha's chattiness, because even on the odd occasions when I evaded it at the front door as she let me in, I had to submit to her torrent of words when she brought me coffee.

Lucie did not always stay with me while I played, not by

any means. She might go shopping or visit friends, and then Mr Mardell would do the honours by coming to drink morning coffee or afternoon tea with me.

Sometimes he asked me to play something, and if he had time he would take me to his room where, with great patience, he tried again and again to teach me to "see" his paintings, as he put it. He never allowed me to echo what he told me. He had no desire to hear his own opinion returned to him in a slightly altered form, he said, making fun, though in flattering terms, of the way I always remembered everything he had said.

"Have the courage to remain silent if you have nothing to say, then you'll grow up to be far less vexatious than most of your sex." He never flagged in his efforts to provide me with an expert analysis of his collection and slowly I developed an eye for it. Once, when we were sitting in his room after one such tour, he asked what had led me to choose the demanding career of a concert pianist.

I explained that nothing seemed more delightful to me than always being able to make music.

"I can understand that, but it's not an easy way to make a living."

He repeated his question and I told him it was because a gentleman had come to our house to play the piano after my little cousin died.

"Jankel Hofer's child?"

"Yes . . . Aron." I realised for the first time how difficult it is to express something in words. I was unable to tell Mr Mardell how much I had loved Aron.

"No-one told me he was ill and when I asked my mother one day whether I could go and play with him again, she said I mustn't talk to anyone about it, but he had been very naughty and so had been sent to a boarding school in England for six months.

"When a person is five years old, six months seems a very long time."

"Yes," Mr Mardell said. "Later the years grow shorter and the hours longer."

He did not allow me to remain silent for long, but asked what I had done after I received that message.

"In the afternoon I went to see my best friend."

"Is she as old as Lucie?" he said, which made me laugh. "Oh no, she's two years younger than I am, but very clever. Much cleverer than me. Even back then. Isn't that funny? We're still friends . . . We walk to school together, and . . ." But Mr Mardell would not let me escape.

"Why did you go to see this clever friend of yours that afternoon?"

"Because I wanted to know when Aron would be coming back. My mother had said 'In exactly six months.' Mili, that's my friend, had a nanny, so I asked her." That had been quite a feat in itself. Should I tell him all about it? Mr Mardell thought I should.

"Mili was playing lotto with her nanny when I came in. Mili was a demon at lotto and she always won. Nanny pretended to be letting her win, but that wasn't true at all. Mili really did win. I went and sat down to join in a little and then I asked nanny: 'What is today plus six months called?' and she asked me if I'd gone mad.

"Nanny wasn't fond of me. She doted on Mili so much that she resented me for being a better piano player than her own sweet darling. Mili outshone me at everything else and she would no doubt have been better at that too, except that she cared little for music.

"Mili said: say exactly what exactly it is you mean!"

"That was really clever," Mr Mardell said.

"Yes, that's what she's like. So I said, 'When it's my birthday it's called the eleventh of March. What's today called and what will today be called in six months from now?' Nanny said, 'Oh, you don't know the names of the months. Mili does. Go on Mili!' And Mili named all the months of the year.

"She slid off her chair and went to stand in her lecturing pose, hands at her back and her left leg forward. It was always a surprise to hear such a deep voice from such a small person.

"'Jan-you-ary,' Mili said.

"'Fe-you-ary.'

"'MARCH,' and then, in one breath, a very long word: "'Junejulyaugustsemberobervembersember.'"

Mr Mardell remarked that that would not have helped me very much. "No, but eventually nanny gave me the right answer after all: today in six months would be the sixth of May, and can I learn to see the paintings again now?"

"Another time," Mr Mardell said. "What happened on the sixth of May?"

"I went to my mother and asked if I could go and meet Aron's train." She turned so pale that the powder on her nose and forehead seemed almost orange in colour. Her dark eyes looked at me with shock and dismay.

"When she understood what I was talking about, my mother said that Aron had now gone to America for ten years, that I was not to write to him nor was I to talk to anyone about him because he'd been so naughty again. I didn't talk to anyone about it, but in the street in front of Aunt Nella's house I bumped into a boy from the neighbourhood right after I'd been playing with Aron's brother. The boy said: 'Have you been playing with the brother of the child who died last year?'"

Mr Mardell said nothing, but because he was sitting at his writing desk he picked up his paper knife and studied it.

"Aron wasn't naughty."

There was no need to tell Mr Mardell that I had lain in bed for several days refusing to eat. I could understand perfectly well that my mother had preferred not to tell me the truth, that she wanted to save me from grief, but I ought not to have believed that Aron had been naughty.

"A few days later the gentleman who played piano came to visit, Monsieur Ercole."

"Really? Him?" Mr Mardell said in disbelief. "I knew him well, in the past. I thought that for many years he . . . Never mind. Go on."

Monsieur Ercole wore a wide, dark cape, and he had a large black slouch hat over his wild white hair. He was accompanied by a robust blonde lady in a dark-blue raincoat. She assured my father that everything would be fine with Monsieur Ercole. After all, he would soon be going home for good and she would come back to fetch him in a couple of hours.

Without his cape and slouch hat, Monsieur Ercole was simply a very small, skinny man, but he had magical hands.

"He sat down at the piano and played. I had no idea anything so beautiful existed in the whole world."

Mr Mardell said he could not imagine it was the first time someone had played the piano in my father's house.

"No, certainly not, people often come to play for us, but

this was quite different, the piece was just like . . . Now you mustn't laugh at me . . ."

"I'm not quick to laugh at anyone."

"It was just like a garden with waterfalls and butterflies in the sun."

"What was it?"

"Chopin's 'First Impromptu'. I kept asking him to play it again and he did, and afterwards he ate with us and then something terrible happened."

"I was waiting for that," Mr Mardell said.

"It was my fault. I asked him when we could come and listen to him giving a concert. He said that he wasn't a concert pianist and that he played only occasionally for good friends and then he set up a terrible screaming. He went purple and foamed at the mouth."

"The poor lad is raving mad," Mr Mardell said. "He thinks his enemies have had him locked up so they can publish a book that he thinks he has written, under their own names."

"It was really very unpleasant and my father had to ring the asylum. When the nurse came to fetch him, Monsieur Ercole lay thrashing about on the floor and she said that now he wouldn't be allowed to go home and it was all my fault."

Then Mr Mardell said something very strange. He said I would have to take great care not to grow up to become a

68

foolish virgin. I had no idea what he meant and he could see that.

"Death is part of life," he said. "And perhaps it's the best part of it and there's no joy without suffering. They're as inseparable as sun and shade." I had experienced profound grief too young and tried to retreat from it into music, and now, unless we watched out, I would in the future be unable to face sorrow or joy with courage and would end up empty-handed like the foolish virgins who had used up all their oil. For an instant he laughed: "The scribes would shake their heads if they heard me; I'll read the parable to you."

While he looked for the place in the bible, which always lay on his desk, he first had to explain to me what a parable was.

I listened enthralled to his calm voice reading out those curious words.

"Then shall the kingdom of heaven be likened unto ten virgins, which took their lamps, and went forth to meet the bridegroom. And five of them were wise, and five were foolish. They that were foolish took their lamps, and took no oil with them: But the wise took oil in their vessels with their lamps. While the bridegroom tarried, they all slumbered and slept. And at midnight there was a cry made, 'Behold, the bridegroom cometh; go ye out to meet him.' Then all those virgins arose, and trimmed their lamps. And the foolish said unto the wise, 'Give us of your oil; for our lamps are gone out.' But the wise answered, saying, 'Not so; lest there be not enough for us and you: but go ye rather to them that sell, and buy for yourselves.' And while they went to buy, the bridegroom came; and they that were ready went in with him to the marriage: and the door was shut. Afterwards came also the other virgins, saying, 'Lord, Lord, open to us.' But He answered and said, 'Verily I say unto you, I know you not.'"

"They're rotters, those wise virgins," I said. "Why not lend the poor souls some oil? Rotten girls they were. I'd rather be a foolish virgin."

"The others are better off in this world," was Mr Mardell's opinion. He looked up. "Don't say anything to Lucie about this; she'll be angry with me for making you sad," he said with a guilty smile. "I ought not to have asked so many questions about Aron." Although as a rule Mr Mardell seemed more sensible than other adults, I knew there was no point in trying to explain to him that this time I was not sad about Aron but about those terrible words: the door was shut; I know you not.

"I'll go and play a bit more," I said.

4

"I'VE ALWAYS ENJOYED TRAVELLING BECAUSE IT'S nice to sit in a train, but for the first time I'm glad to have arrived somewhere," I said to Lucie one morning. She sighed, "Oh, how complicated and difficult you're being again."

It was not the first time I had made a cautious attempt to tell her how wonderful I found it to be with her in the quiet room where the grand piano was kept. Having failed, I gave up. Perhaps she did not want to understand and nothing could be worse than annoying her. Just imagine if she should say: don't bother coming back; or: another child is going to be playing the piano here; or: I no longer have time for you.

It seemed there were two sorts of people in the world, ordinary ones with whom you could talk and rare ones to whom you just had to listen. Not that Lucie was talkative. When she was in the room she would sit with her sweet blonde head bent over some needlework; she really only chatted to me when Bertha brought coffee or when her father was with us. After our disagreement about the wise and foolish virgins I did not see him for several days, but now he came upstairs again and we pretended it had never happened. With him I could talk, and I told him that the previous day I had made a strange discovery. A lady had come to visit my grandmother. She asked me, as everyone did, what I thought of Antwerp and I answered, as always, that it was a beautiful city and as I was speaking I realised I knew nothing of it, aside from a few rooms in a few houses, which was really quite ridiculous when I had been there so often.

After listening to me with his usual civility, Mr Mardell said, "If I understand you correctly, you'd like to see something of the city. Well, we have an in-house specialist on the subject. Gabriel. What that lad doesn't know about Antwerp is impossible to say. I'll ask him to come up." Lucie said she would go and fetch him, and while she was gone Mr Mardell told me that Gabriel was remarkably gifted in all kinds of ways. "Where he gets it from goodness knows, not from his parents at any rate. Born in the gutter and raised on a dung heap." Gabriel entered the room, looking shy.

"Sit down, Gabriel," Mr Mardell said. "We have a serious problem. Our young friend has discovered that although she has often been here, she knows nothing at all about our city, where, if I'm not mistaken, she was born." I was able to confirm the fact. "Now, we have agreed that this state of affairs cannot go on any longer, which is why I've called for you. You are to make a list for her of the buildings she must go and see." Gabriel blushed with pleasure.

"Oh, it's such a delightful city, my child, with so many beautiful sights, for a start . . ."

I interrupted him: "I would like it very much, Gabriel, if you were to make a list for me, but there's no hurry, because after all I'm not allowed out alone, and everyone is always far too busy to go with me."

"Then I'll accompany you," Lucie said firmly. "Ask at home whether you can go for a walk with me on Sunday afternoon and if Gabriel has the time and the inclination then perhaps he'll come with us to explain everything. I'd like to learn more about the city myself. How is it by the way, Gabriel, that you know so much?"

"When you love something," Gabriel said, blushing, "you want to learn everything about it. Every week I read a book about Antwerp. You'd be surprised, Miss Mardell, how much has been written about it, going back many years."

"But how do you get hold of all those expensive books?" asked Lucie.

"There is such a thing as a library, dear child," Mr Mardell observed.

"So I have heard," Lucie said indignantly. "But by the time

Gabriel has finished work here, it's been shut for hours."

"Yes, Miss Mardell, that's true, but in the library there's a young lady who chooses books for me and takes them home with her, so that I can fetch them in the evenings and return them after I've read them."

"That's absurd, really, when I have so much time," Lucie decided. "From now on, if Gittel and I become your pupils, so to speak, then I insist on going to fetch the books for you."

"That would be so kind of you, Miss Mardell, but I hardly dare to accept."

Mr Mardell stood up and stroked Gabriel's hair. "I'd just go along with it if I were you, young man," he said. "My daughter is at a loss what to do with her time. Good day to you, ladies, we're off back to work." He laid his arm loosely around Gabriel's shoulders as they left the room.

"Your father is very good to Gabriel, isn't he?"

"Oh yes," Lucie said. "He's exceptionally fond of him. It seems Gabriel has a great head for business. Now just you go on playing."

It took me a great deal of trouble to gain permission to go for a walk with Lucie that Sunday afternoon; I felt it was best not to say anything about Gabriel coming with us. My mother would have forbidden it outright, but Grandmother was always torn when it came to the Mardells. The faithful Rosalba, who took my side, settled the matter. "Oh, let her go," she said. "It's very boring for her here, really. Fredie and Charlie are too old and the other children far too young for her. She's a bit left out whatever she does and I'm sure she's not going to learn anything bad from that nice Miss Mardell."

My mother declared that she failed to understand what I saw in that elderly damsel. "How old must she be? She could be your mother." Yes, she was indeed ancient, twenty-nine, which in fact made her friendship all the more valuable to me, but no-one needed to know that.

When Lucie came to fetch me that Sunday she was all smiles for five minutes with my grandmother and the moment the front door fell shut behind us we hurried to the first side street, where Gabriel was waiting. He had only one suit, the black one he wore to the office, but for the walk he had got himself a flat straw hat and a green bow tie.

"Oh, Gabriel," Lucie said, even before I could greet him. "Take that ugly thing off your head. What possessed you? It looks hideous." He blushed to the roots of his hair and threw the unfortunate hat down on the road. He refused to pick it up again. "Is the tie wrong too?" he ventured. Lucie tilted her head and, with her eyes half shut, she studied the bow tie.

"Too green," was her eventual verdict. "But don't go throwing it away, please, or I'll never dare say anything to you in future." They both laughed at that until tears came to their eyes.

Lucie said she had brought some chocolate for me and I understood and admired her tact. She knew I was always stuffed like a fattened goose by Rosalba before I went out, so that for the sake of the family's honour I would be incapable of squeezing in a single mouthful elsewhere. After I had refused the chocolate bars, Lucie was able to ask Gabriel to take them off her hands without hurting his pride. He devoured them; he was always hungry, he said.

"That's because you're still growing," Lucie teased and Gabriel told her that a man of twenty-three had no more growing to do.

"Now, first we're going to the cathedral," he said. "Have you ever been inside it, Gittel?" I had never been anywhere.

Gabriel claimed that the Cathedral of Our Lady in Antwerp had the most beautiful statue of the Virgin in the whole world, and Lucie asked how he could possibly know, since he had never visited any foreign country. Gabriel answered that he had seen pictures of other Virgins and their faces were sickly sweet and boring compared to the mysterious, austere face of "our own".

"She isn't ours," Lucie said. "We're not Catholics."

But according to Gabriel she belonged to everyone who was born in Antwerp. They would have gone on quarrelling about that had Gabriel not at once added that it was only because of an unhappy accident that he was a native of Antwerp. On the way to Canada his family had been housed in emigrants' lodgings at the harbour and when his father went out to buy something to eat he was run down by a dray cart. "He was killed on the spot and because of the shock I was born two months early. My mother no longer wanted to go to Canada after that, although how she managed to get permission to stay here I don't understand to this day." He sighed. "My mother is a spirited woman. She raised me and my sisters on her own and she still works herself to death for us. She can't seem to stop, even though she has no need to now that my sisters are married and I've got a good job."

"Bunkum," Lucie said. "I've always thought my father keeps you on far too low a salary and not only you, Salvinia and Menie too. With starvation wages like that the poor things might be engaged for eternity. I'm going to have to tell Father the truth to his face."

Gabriel begged her not to interfere. "He teaches us to think and act for ourselves. Anyone who works under his guidance for two years learns more of the trade than he would in a dozen years at one of the big banks."

Lucie shrugged.

It was mild spring weather and in the Sunday-hushed streets our shadows trotted animatedly ahead of us over the bumpy cobbles. We walked in the road so that it was easier for Gabriel to show us the buildings he regarded as important and I felt sorry for Lucie. She was proud of her small, narrow feet and always wore high-heeled, elegant little shoes that showed off her fine ankles and arched instep – far from suitable footwear for tackling the city's notorious heavy cobblestones. She was no doubt suffering in silence, but she kept up a brave front.

The cathedral tower was invisible, spun about with a cobweb of scaffolding.

Gabriel first took us to the grey Matsys Well, next to the cathedral, of which the wrought ironwork was also, or so he said, among the most beautiful in the world.

"Love made the blacksmith into a painter," Lucie deciphered from the letters chiselled into the stone of the well. "What will love make of you, Gabriel?"

"A fool," he said. "That happened long ago, incidentally," and the look he gave her with his blue eyes was so angry and hard that I was shocked. What was this monkey of a boy thinking that he dared to look daggers at Lucie? She was so sweet, she merely smiled in response. "Well, you do talk a lot of nonsense," she said.

Gabriel looked at the ground. The sunlight fired sparks

from his auburn hair and his dark eyelashes were so inordinately long that they threw shadows like fans across his thin cheeks.

"A guide who gives conducted tours is expected to talk a lot of nonsense. It goes with the job," was his terse reply. "I'll make sure, however, that you have no further grounds for complaint."

When we were inside the cathedral he showed us a long narrow copper strip laid diagonally across the flagstones. "That's what's called a meridian; at twelve noon, the sun shines on it through an opening in that window." He pointed out to us the hole in the window and I was impressed by his wealth of knowledge. Gabriel told us that fate was smiling on us, since the curtains had been opened to reveal the triptych "The Descent from the Cross", painted by Rubens, whereas very often they were closed.

"And you'll no doubt tell us it's the most beautiful triptych in the world, isn't that right, Gabriel," Lucie teased him in a whisper.

"I'm not the only one who says so, anybody who has the remotest clue about painting knows it is." He sounded cross. He said that the colours in it gleamed like precious jewels and I felt guilty, because I could not see the beauty of the imposing work.

The cathedral was empty, apart from a few sightseers and

those grief-stricken, afflicted, praying women who are to be found in any church at any hour of the day. Antwerp's Our Lady was dressed in a robe of blue brocade with countless pearls stitched into it, and the Christ child on her arm wore a huge silver crown out of all proportion to its body.

"The only thing you'll remember of all this magnificence," Gabriel whispered, "is the pale, mysterious face of Our Lady."

Lucie thought her expression too stern and Gabriel, who seemed to know everything, said, "Yes, she is stern. She's not satisfied with a prayer if it comes from the lips alone; for her, words need to be spoken from the heart," and Lucie muttered that he was such a strange boy, wasn't he? I was glad to be out walking along the sunny streets again; the smell of incense and the holy silence under the high vaulted roof had in some strange way made me feel oppressed and sad.

"One of the curious things about this city has always been that it understands both workers and dreamers," Gabriel said. "Everyone here has ended up in the right place, according to their nature: those who stand with both feet on the ground, and the rest who live with their heads in the clouds." He told us the painter of the triptych had been a confidant of the king and that even as a very old man he had managed to marry the most beautiful young girl in the city.

"Who therefore, just as he deserved, cheated on him left right and centre," Lucie sneered and they bickered on that subject for another few minutes. My pleasure in the walk was somewhat marred by the way they were displaying irritation with each other all the time, for no reason. I could understand it of Lucie, her feet must be hurting her, but I thought Gabriel outrageously rude to let fly at her time and again. Mr Mardell ought to have heard him. He would have smartly put him in his place.

Lucie had far too much patience with the impudent boy. Now she was asking him whether he thought he was one of the city's workers or one of its dreamers.

"I must be a worker," Gabriel said. "I've no objection to that and I'm glad I've ended up in the banking trade, because it has been making an important contribution to the city's wealth and status for a very long time. I'd have liked even better to have something to do with the port, but I was never given the opportunity."

He took us to the River Scheldt, where the current was slow and the surface reflected the mother-of-pearl of the light spring sky. I was accustomed to the sea, so the breadth of the river disappointed me, but I made no mention of that because Gabriel was telling us about big ships that came to the river from far and wide, laden with fragrant spices, ivory, gold and expensive kinds of timber.

"I had been wondering," Lucie said , "how it was that we came to have so many ivory and gold houses here." Gabriel gave her a furious look and said it was easy to laugh at everything. He spoke about citizens of the city who left to work abroad but could not forget Antwerp and who always, when they were old, returned to bring her the most beautiful or important of the treasures they had collected on their travels, because they each wanted to do something for her in their turn to add to her lustre. "Like the way the old painter kept adorning his bride with different flowers and jewels to accentuate her radiant blonde beauty." The corners of his mouth trembled with repressed laughter as he said it and I expected Lucie to be angry again, but she asked him in her sweetest voice whether he too had plans to enhance the glory of the city. "I'm a poor Jewish foreigner," Gabriel said, "and I love this city as only a person who is poor and Jewish and a foreigner can love. You won't understand that, Miss Lucie. For people who live in big houses with beautiful gardens, the buildings and parks of the city are less important than they are for a poor boy like me, and the love of a foreigner who knows he'll soon have to move on is always more intense than that of a person who knows he'll be able to stay with his love for ever. Still, the gratitude of a Jew to a place where he is not subjected to persecution must be something even you can understand."

"It's not true, what you say," Lucie said. "I went to school with girls whose forebears did great things for this city. Their love was even fiercer than yours."

"Perhaps you're right," Gabriel said. "But meanwhile I'm still a poor Jewish foreigner who will never be able to do anything for this city. Unattainable ambitions seem to be my fate."

"For you nothing need be unattainable," said the truly angelic Lucie. "If only you were a bit more courageous and could muster a bit more self-confidence." I thought he had more than enough self-confidence, and I was glad when he said he had to go home. "I promised my mother I'd paint the kitchen cupboard and line the shelves with linoleum. Next week I'll have more time. Good day, Miss Mardell. Bye, Gittel." He shook hands with each of us and raced off as if the devil was at his heels.

"He must be terrified of his mother to run away like a mad thing," I said. Lucie did not reply and we walked in silence to my grandmother's house. When we got there, Lucie asked whether I had enjoyed the walk sufficiently to undertake another next week. "You were so quiet," she said. "I thought you were bored." No, I had not been bored and I very much wanted to go with them again. I waved until the tall door of her house closed behind her.

On the way home I had been contemplating what to tell my family about the outing. They were playing whist. They asked absently where I had been and I told them I had walked along the Scheldt with Miss Mardell. I thought it best to say nothing about the visit to the cathedral. Rosalba was darning stockings and she was the only one to respond to my account. She whispered that she could tell I had had a wonderful afternoon just by looking at me and that she would help me to get permission for the next walk.

Her help turned out to be sorely needed, because on Sunday there was drizzly rain and my grandmother predicted double pneumonia for Lucie and me if we went out walking in it.

Lucie promised to deliver me back dry as a bone. "We'll go by tram to the museum and then I'll take her for a cup of tea." Rosalba kept her word and came to our aid by saying the rain had stopped, and after Lucie had exhibited her usual five minutes of affability we at last got out onto the street.

"Do you always have such trouble when you want to go somewhere?" she said. "How can you stand it?"

Well, I was unable to say, never having thought about it before.

Gabriel must have been on the lookout for us at his corner for some time, because his hair was soaking wet. After we greeted each other, Lucie began telling him that she had been thinking about his final remark of the week before. I was pleased to hear her say she thought it was pure poppycock.

"My great-grandfather came here as a foreigner too and you know how far he got."

"Those were different times," Gabriel said. "And he was already rich when he arrived. In any case, he must have been far cleverer in business than I am."

"My father says you have a great aptitude for it."

"Really?" Gabriel blushed yet again, this time with pride. "Who knows, maybe I'll be a famous banker yet. Recently someone from England came to the office. He asked me whether I wanted to go and work for him. Maybe I will. The prospects were glowing. Then when I've earned a lot of money I'll come back and have a big house built, full of art-works, and when I die I'll bequeath it to the city."

He said I too must do something for my native city and I promised, magnanimously, to come and give a concert every year in aid of a good cause, as soon as I became the most famous pianist in Europe. At that point we asked Lucie what she was going to do. "I'm fit only to be a good audience," she said. "I'll come and admire Gabriel's palace, if he still wants to know me, that is, and I'll sit in the front row and clap very hard at that concert of yours."

The museum turned out to be shut and we took a tram to the Scheldt, which looked dismal and drab in the rain.

"Now even you surely can't think much of your beloved city," laughed Lucie, but Gabriel said a little rain could not make his city any less dear to him, since that would be just as unfaithful as suddenly ceasing to love someone because they were unfortunate enough to have caught a cold.

With further tourism impossible, Lucie suggested treating ourselves to waffles in the café on the quayside. We were the only customers and the rain poured in rivulets down the tall windows, making the brightly lit premises, decorated with many mirrors, doubly cosy. A sleepy old waiter in a green apron brought us a pile of waffles on a brass tray; hot, brittle and delicious they were, thickly dusted with icing sugar that was speckled grey by the fat. "Just like a yellow doorstep with thawing snow, if you half close your eyes," I remarked to Gabriel and the next moment I spat all that remained in my mouth onto the plate in disgust. Gabriel asked if it was a hair or a stone, but I had tasted the sin through the innocent vanilla flavour of the icing sugar. Lucie furrowed her almost invisible eyebrows and chided that I was too old to do such a revolting thing, but there had been no other choice when I realised the waffles could not be kosher, indeed they were very probably made with lard.

Gabriel showed understanding for the situation and said, to comfort me, that Our Lord would not blame me this time because I had committed the sin unwittingly, but Lucie let out a mocking, provocative laugh: "You've eaten four and you found them very nice, didn't you?" "Delicious," I had to admit, feeling dejected. "Then I'd eat the last one as well," she said. "If you've sinned four times then a fifth won't matter all that much, or don't you dare?" I shared the last waffle with Gabriel. Sinning deliberately was far from easy.

Lucie was buoyant. She teased Gabriel and me by turns and said the craziest things, such as: "Next week we're going to Lier to look at the beguinage. Then I can arrange for a room right away because it's about time." She explained to me that only old, unmarried women lived in the beguinage, and Gabriel stood up and said he had promised his mother to paint the staircase. I asked if he had decided not to go with us to Lier. He said, "Oh I'll go, why not? But I don't like nonsensical talk." He sat down again and frowned at the crumbs on his plate. Lucie asked the waiter to order a taxi. She had promised, after all, that I would not get wet.

She delivered me as arranged and left with Gabriel, who on arrival at Grandmother's house had crouched down on the floor of the taxi. She would take him home too, Lucie said, because he had come out without a coat.

I had not been on the island since meeting Lucie, and even Klembem, the spider man, had been lying low. The next morning I heard his nasty piping voice again for the first time. Klembem lived at the top of a mountain near the North Pole, in a spider's web with threads as thick as steel cables. He had the body and legs of a spider, only far, far bigger. The legs ended in human hands and he had a human head in which blood-red eyes sparkled. I felt his chilling, poisonous breath on my neck when I heard Mr Mardell give Lucie a scolding in the hallway because Gabriel was ill. She ought to have known better, he said sternly, than to let a poor boy with weak lungs walk around in the rain for hours. When I came to her aid, saying in earnest that all we had done was to eat waffles in a café where it was lovely and warm and that Lucie had even taken Gabriel home in a taxi, it only seemed to annoy him all the more and I heard Klembem's miserable snickering laugh. "Now it's going nice and wrong for you here," Klembem said. "You were far too comfy as it was."

"Don't worry, Father," Lucie said. "Gabriel really will come back and work here again."

When Gabriel was still sick two days later she asked whether I thought it would be a nice idea to visit him, enquire after his health, and take him some sweets. "There's no point even asking at home," I said. "They'd be far too afraid of infection."

"We can go this morning," Lucie said. "What's done is done."

"Then I needn't even tell anyone . . ."

"You know best," Lucie said. "What would he enjoy eating, do you think?" She went to the kitchen and came back a little later with a shopping bag full of sardines, salmon and compote. I had just enough money to buy a few lemons, which my grandmother always said were the only effective remedy for a cold. Lucie told me she had not thought of lemons, and that it was a good plan. We went downstairs and immediately ran into Mr Mardell, who had just accompanied one of his clients to the door.

"At Gittel's insistence we're to undertake a work of charity," Lucie said, and she pinched me so hard in the left upper arm that it was all I could do to stifle a yelp. "We're going to see Gabriel, laden with lemons – that's Gittel's idea too."

"Give him warm greetings from me and tell him to get well soon," Mr Mardell said. "You can also say" – he hesitated for a moment – "ah well, yes, you may as well tell him, it might cheer him up a little, that he must do his best to get better quickly because I have some far from unpleasant news for him." "What is it, Father?" Lucie said, but Mr Mardell claimed that women were incapable of keeping a secret. "What I have to tell him, I'll tell the lad myself."

Under Lucie's guidance I bought my contribution to Gabriel's recovery and we had to take another taxi because I would need to be home by the usual time if our outing was to remain undiscovered.

The street where we stopped at a vegetable market looked

miserable. The lemons were on sale at a far lower price than I would have had to pay in the expensive shop that Lucie frequented, yet despite that, mine were much bigger and better looking.

"He lives up there on the first floor with his mother," Lucie said. She tugged at a black-painted bell-pull and we had to wait for a moment. A sash window slid open and a loud female voice asked who we were and what we wanted. Lucie seemed struck dumb and I had just started speaking on her behalf when the invisible owner of the voice called out that she could already see and would open the door. We entered the house and climbed a steep, unpainted staircase lined with newspaper by way of a stair carpet.

"Gabriel was supposed to paint the stairs, remember?" Lucie said. "He didn't get very far." The top three steps had been neatly painted light grey.

Klembem almost tumbled out of his web with laughter, because at the top of the stairs stood Grandma Hofer. In dismay I dropped the bag of lemons. The paper tore and I ran after the escaped fruits, which hopped downstairs exasperatingly far apart like three cheeky yellow goblins. When I got back upstairs, out of breath, I found Lucie stammering at Grandma Hofer, who let her go on for a while before saying, "But I'm *not* Gabriel's mother. She's cleaning the living room. She wasn't expecting such exalted company at this hour of the day." We stood packed together in a narrow, dark hallway full of a miserable smell of cabbage and washing. We heard bumping noises behind one of the two doors. "She must be ready by now," Grandma Hofer said before shouting, "We're coming!" She opened the door nearer to the front of the house and beckoned us to follow her into what turned out to be a long, narrow room.

Gabriel was lying with bright-red cheeks and shining eyes beneath a mountain of blankets on a camp bed by the window. A pale, thin woman with grey hair stood next to him, a mop in her bony hands. She was no less abashed than we were. She said we must sit down and, after mumbling something about making tea, walked straight out of the door.

"How are you doing, Gabriel?" Lucie said in a husky voice. "My father sends his heartfelt greetings and says to tell you he has pleasant news for you when you get better."

"A raise," Grandma Hofer said. "And if you want my honest opinion, it ought to have happened far sooner."

In the middle of the room was an oversized square table with six chairs planted formally around it. The wall with the door was otherwise completely taken up by a tall old-fashioned sideboard that had panes of glass in a chequered pattern of alternating red and green. Close to the opposite wall was a pot-bellied stove, stoked up red hot. On the table, which was spread with a white crocheted cloth, sat a dish with a roasted chicken and a large jar of aspic.

Lucie unpacked her bag. "We've got some delicious things for you, Gabriel," she said. "And Gittel has bought lemons for you with her own money."

Gabriel, who looked even more like his angel namesake than usual, thanked us in a whisper.

"You should hold your tongue," Grandma Hofer said. "You've got a cold on your vocal cords, which means speaking is strictly forbidden. Plus the fact that I've just filled you up with lime-blossom tea." She turned to Lucie: "You know, the only remedy for a cold is sweating and pissing and then more sweating and pissing!" Lucie blanched. She wasn't used to Grandma Hofer the way Gabriel and I were. He seemed untroubled by her and murmured, "Don't be so bossy, Aunt Lea, or I won't eat a bite of that delectable chicken."

Grandma Hofer laughed and pulled his hair. I needed to speak or I would burst with curiosity.

"Is Grandma Hofer your aunt, Gabriel?"

He shook his head. "No, not a real aunt, but the best, the only friend to my mother and me . . ."

"Be quiet now!" Grandma Hofer barked. "I'm capable of answering all cheeky questions myself. Go ahead, Gittel, can I be of any further assistance? Just say, but first I'll say something to you. I'm sure your grandmother is unaware that you're here. I know her. Never in life would she allow it. They're all raving *meshuga* in that house. If they could, they would keep you under a bell-jar. Pooh." She knew I could not contradict her.

All four of us fell silent until Gabriel's mother reappeared, but by that time I had determined, to my own amazement, that Grandma Hofer looked quite different here from when she was with Grandmother. It was the first time I had seen her without a hat. She almost always wore a strange type of headgear, black with a cockade on one side; my grandmother claimed a slave must dwell in a cavern somewhere who did nothing but make hats for Grandma Hofer and that if the slave ever died then the manufacturing of them would, happily, become one of the lost arts. It also occurred to me that I did not know how old Grandma Hofer was. To me she was ageless, just like Grandmother and Rosalba.

Gabriel's mother was carrying a tin tray with a teapot and glasses on it. She set it down on the table and gave us each a glass of tea. Grandma Hofer proposed "slaughtering" the jar of aspic. She did not wait for an answer but busily fetched plates from the sideboard onto each of which she flung a generous blob. It tasted surprisingly good. Gabriel had to keep the blankets pulled up and Grandma Hofer fed him the aspic as if he were a small child. He was not afraid of her in the least. He even playfully bit her hand. "Ungrateful scoundrel," she said, laughing. "You little monkey, watch out, or I'll put you across my knee."

"It wouldn't be the first time," the hoarse Gabriel said.

"No, we've known each other for quite a while and soon it'll be time for you to think about marriage. I've got a treasure of a girl in mind for you. Not yet eighteen and with a nice little nest-egg. I'm for marrying young and with someone of your own kind. You mustn't end up with such a bad match as my pig-headed sons who refused to listen to me."

Gabriel's mother then became talkative. In a sorrowful voice she told us how desperate she had been with the new-born Gabriel, in a hospital in a strange country where she did not know the language, and then a miracle had happened. She suddenly remembered that an old schoolfriend of hers must be living in this city. Fortunately one of the nuns caring for her turned out to be Polish and with great difficulty the woman managed to trace the address and deliver a note. Not an hour after receiving it, Grandma Hofer was at her bedside with clothes and food and everything you could imagine. Grandma Hofer took up the tale: "And that whippersnapper there – you'd never think it of him now – was the most beautiful baby I'd seen in all my born days. The nuns said: 'Just like the Little Baby Jesus.' *Lehavdil*. And since that day I've treated him as my third son."

"*Lehavdil*" was murmured whenever anyone, by accident, compared a healthy person with a sick one, or someone living with someone dead. In itself it was an innocent Hebrew word that meant nothing more than "to make a distinction", but it seemed that if you said it quickly enough after such a slip of the tongue it appeased any evil spirits that might be present. I could tell from Lucie's startled face that she had understood nothing of Grandma Hofer's last few statements. I would explain it all to her outside. She stood up. "It's time to go, Gittel. Bye, Gabriel, get well soon."

Grandma Hofer allowed us only to wave to him. Looking despondent, his mother shook our hands and said that although her life was hard, she felt amazed and thankful every single day that there were still so many good people in the world. But she had a voice that turned every kind word into a lament or a reproach.

Grandma Hofer accompanied us to the stairs and there she grabbed me by the chin and forced me to look her straight in the eye. "If you hold your tongue, so will I," she said. That was a great relief, but despite it Lucie cried in the taxi, and because I failed to understand why, I could not comfort her.

By the end of the week Gabriel was back at work and he came to thank Lucie and me formally for our visit. He said he was glad to be well enough to go with us to Lier on Sunday.

5

OUR VISITS TO ANTWERP FOLLOWED A SET PATTERN:
when time for the baroness came round, I knew the end was
near. Even if we were in Grandmother's good books when
we arrived, it was usually only for a short time because my
mother could not refrain from squabbling mightily with
Uncle Fredie, who was Grandmother's youngest child and
the apple of her eye. The continual attacks on her favourite
in-furiated her and without saying a word she always managed to make it plain when her appreciation of our presence
in her household had reached rock bottom. There was then
no choice but to be in her house only during the night and in
daytime to honour each of the aunts in turn with a visit.
Soon they would have had enough of us too.

When that point was reached we took up our final position: Baroness Bommens.

This time, because of my friendship with Lucie, I had

been paying little attention to the inevitable course of events. She accompanied me to Grandmother's front door as usual and said I would do well to plead right away for permission to go to Lier, but as soon as I was inside the house I knew that I might as well spare myself the trouble. We were already in the middle of the principal scene of the final act.

At the top of the stairs that led to the living rooms stood Grandmother, Uncle Fredie and my mother who, deploying her own dramatic arts, declared, "I'm not staying here a day longer, not a day, do you understand? Tomorrow we're going home. Come with me, Gittel, we're off to the baroness. At least we'll be treated warmly there and not like the dregs of society."

"Beautiful baroness," Fredie sneered. "Baroness with the left hand, and a fine baron: Baron Zeep."*

He spoke that last word, which means soap, with a heavy Flemish accent, so that it sounded something like "*zieyep*". I didn't understand any of this, but I knew I had seen the last of the quiet hours in Lucie's house and the pleasant walks with her and Gabriel.

My mother descended the stairs like an insulted monarch and made a long performance of putting on her hat. Rosalba

* "Baron Zeep" was a term in popular use in the 1920s as a sarcastic reference to those who had made good money out of the German occupation during the First World War.

appeared at the bottom of the steps to the kitchen. "Don't be so silly," she said. "You haven't eaten yet." "Then we'll starve," my mother said gloomily. "I'll be glad when we're found famished in the gutter; then you'll have reason to be deeply ashamed."

I was less keen on the prospect, as Grandmother could tell. "You're the one who should be ashamed," she said. "Upsetting the child like that. Come on, back upstairs, the evening meal will be ready shortly."

She strode proudly into the dining room, followed by Fredie. My mother hung her hat back on the hallstand and I was amazed to see that she was shaking with laughter.

She pointed at the mirror and in it I saw myself: fat as a bear. A good many months would have to pass before I could be fished out of a gutter in an emaciated state.

At the table not a word was spoken, except by Rosalba and me. Grandmother stared sternly ahead and Uncle Fredie and my mother sulked with all their might.

Whenever we went to see the baroness I was given furlough from the navy. Where my mother got her nautical preference from I will never know, but until I was fifteen she had me go about only ever in sailor suits. In summer they were made of white cotton and in winter a scratchy navy-blue woollen fabric. I also possessed a party dress of blue taffeta that I was allowed to wear on very rare occasions. The baroness would have been displeased with my mother to say the least had we failed to appear before her in our Sun-day best. She and her daughter, Madame Odette, wore silk, velvet and lace. They glistened with jewels and were not averse to a little fur and ostrich feathers.

The baroness' grandsons were invariably dressed in velvet suits with lace collars, silk sashes around their horrid waists. The little dolts wore their mousy hair in long ponytails at their foreheads and corkscrew curls to their shoulders. From between those embellishments little pale-blue eyes looked slyly out at the world. They were my age and they walked off shrieking as soon as they saw me. But they usually reappeared as soon as the cakes were passed around.

Other than that, the visit to the baroness was one big party. Even the long walk to reach her was enjoyable from start to finish, because the palace where she lived stood out among the other houses in the avenue from a long way off by having all its windows hung with net curtains in a variety of pastel hues.

The baroness liked to speak of the blue salon, the red reception room, and so on. She had furnished each room in its own colour and even the windows were dressed accordingly.

"Taste is taste," she said. "And I'm satisfied with mine." I felt she had a right to be. In my view none of the other houses

I visited had a decor that could match hers in beauty and distinction, richness and elegance.

Madame Odette, in blue *moiré*, flanked by her two Fauntleroys, was already standing outside the front door to await our arrival. We had barely got any closer before the two little blighters ran yelling and screaming into the house.

"Please excuse that," their mother said with resignation. "It's all so difficult . . . For a woman alone . . . With two of those scallywags . . . To bring them up properly." She heaved a deep sigh; each of her short sentences was introduced with a sigh. "How is Mama doing?" my mother asked.

"The same as ever. Remarkable for her age. *Femme du monde*. To her last gasp."

A servant took our coats and Madame Odette said, "Today Mama will receive you in the boudoir because Gittel so admired it the last time, and Arnold says you must not be allowed to leave before he has seen you."

Arnold was her older brother and it was thanks to his mediation that we found ourselves in these noble circles. He had been apprenticed to the firm in which my father began his far from successful career in trade, at around the same time. Arnold Bommens had made it somewhat further in life; he owned one of those superbly run bars that are correctly said to be goldmines. In such a distinguished milieu this tended to go unmentioned. On odd occasions something was said to Arnold in tones of reproach about "Noblesse oblige". Bommens was an affable, jovial man, and as far as I was concerned he had a historical mystique, in that his was the only truly pockmarked face I had ever seen. I was unable to take my eyes off it.

He was genuinely fond of my father, and the warm affection audible in his voice when he asked after him and talked about "old times" always did me good.

What had confused me rather on my first visit was that everyone in the house was called Bommens, the baroness herself, "our" Mr Arnold, Madame Odette, and Lucien and Robert as well. Sometimes a granddaughter stayed with them, the child of another daughter who lived in Ghent, and she was a Hubertineke Bommens. This peerage was inherited through the female line.

Madame Odette was a sturdy, red-haired woman with a voluptuous figure. I thought her too ample, but Rubens would have enjoyed painting her. We walked behind her down a long hallway lined with black-and-white marble tiles and then had to climb a few stairs to enter the baroness' blue boudoir. The room had won my admiration above all for the large painting hanging in it. I greeted the baroness and despite everything Mr Mardell had taught me I went to stand right in front of it.

". . . and she just goes on looking at the huntsman," the

baroness said with her strange, nebulous voice. "You watch out, child, you watch out."

The painting showed a clearing in a forest. To the left lay a girl without many clothes on, sleeping in an elegant but uncomfortable position. Leaning over her, a gentleman in a green hunting costume looked down. At the bottom of the heavy gilded frame was a bronze plate on which was inscribed: "Will he now cause her to wake? Alas, no."

During an earlier visit I had been incautious enough to ask "Why is that?" and the horrible grown-up laugh of which I was always a little afraid had made the cups tinkle on the marble tabletop. There was much to be seen in each of the baroness' rooms, but this one surpassed them all. Everything was light blue or gold. There were two mirrors that reached from floor to ceiling, a dressing table covered in little crystal bottles and caskets, and a Récamier couch. Four gold angels were climbing down from the ceiling on a gold chain, each of them holding a rose made of glass in which light bulbs were concealed that emitted a dim, gentle light.

"When a woman gets a little older she needs to avoid bright light," the baroness said, and in the half-dark she did indeed look spirited despite her eighty years. She always reminded me of a powdered Pekingese with her large, round, protruding eyes and very short and broad *retroussé* nose, and also because like that breed of dog she was forever moistening her lower lip with her tongue. Three black curls fell onto her forehead from below a white lace mantilla draped gracefully over her head and shoulders.

This visit once again took place according to a fixed routine. As soon as we were sitting down the house servant came in with a tray of cakes and sweets, and Madame Odette poured hot chocolate from a large blue jug. That was the moment at which the two little noblemen barged in and clamoured for their share. There were always the same kind of cakes, high and long with three layers of mocha filling inside, decorated with silver balls to look like dominoes. As a guest I was always given the double six, with twelve silver balls, to the fury and frustration of Lucien and Robert. To my relief they always disappeared to their own rooms with their haul and only then did things get really cosy. A plump white cat, which had come in with the servant, lay purring in the baroness' satin lap as she sat close to the large gas heater. I was staring drowsily at the flames when Odette remarked, with a succession of sighs, "A woman such as I. Experiences her hell. Already here on earth." I felt she had nothing to complain of in that lovely warm room with all those tasty things to eat and beautiful clothes, and since Lucien and Robert were her own children she could surely not find them so very unpleasant.

"Don't you ever hear from him at all?" my mother said.

"Never," was the answer. "After Robert was born, he left. Not a sign of life from him since. Hide nor hair."

Whoever he may have been, in my heart I found it hard to blame him.

". . . and then when I think of Papa . . .!" Odette sighed.

"I always tell Odette there's no man on earth these days to compare to the baron. Such virtue. Such nobility." The baroness began sobbing with indignation and thrust the cat from her lap. It gave her a resentful look and lay down to toast its belly nicely in front of the gas fire.

"The ground I walked on was too hard," the baroness went on. "Every day red roses with my breakfast. Every month a magnificent jewel on the date of our first meeting. He would have brought me the moon on a gold platter if I'd asked him. I never did ask for it, but I know he would!"

I felt very much like asking her how she thought the baron could have manoeuvred such a big dish, moon and all, in through the front door, but the baroness began wailing louder and louder.

"Aaaah," she cried. "Aaah. It's upon me again, my *crise de nerfs*, my *crise de nerfs*. Quick, Odette, my smelling salts, my powders, or I'll expire at your feet."

To distract her a little I said in a pitying tone, "The dear baron who was so good to you, was that Baron Zieyep?"

This proved an effective remedy. The *crise de nerfs* ceased at once. The baroness got up out of her chair like a goddess of vengeance and Madame Odette turned purple.

"What was that you said?" "She didn't think that up herself." They spoke in unison, casting poisonous looks at my poor mother, who blushed to the roots of her hair.

"Zil-yeb," my mother said, with a noticeable pause between the two syllables. "Zilyeb. The child is confused. We have a friend, a Polish baron, who occasionally comes to our house and now she thinks that every baron is called Baron 'Zil-yeb'."

The baroness sat down again and opted for the wiser course. "That must be it, then," she said with feigned detachment. Odette was not so easy. In sugary tones she asked, holding the dish of sweets out to me, "And what sort of a gentleman is he, then, this Polish baron. What does he look like?" I was at a complete loss, but just then "our" Bommens came into the room like an angel of salvation.

"Ah, all the ladies together. Excellent. *Bonjour Maman*, hello my dear Thea, it does me good to see you. So, little Odette . . . And look, who is that big young lady over there? Surely it can't be our Gittel? Oh, what a shame. I've brought a bunny for her, but she's no doubt far too big for that now."

He laid an Easter bunny on the table in front of me. The blessed creature was carrying a basket of eggs on its back.

"Oh no, Uncle Arnold. Oh no, I'm not too big at all." I

threw myself at his neck and kissed his pockmarked cheeks exuberantly. In normal circumstances I was too shy to do that, but I realised I had said one of those mysterious things that make grown-ups angry and that his presence had spared me a good deal of unpleasantness.

Much to my regret we did not this time wait for the second round of treats (crème de menthe for the ladies, lemonade for me, and sandwiches).

"Come now, what's all this?" Arnold protested. "I take the trouble to get home early and already you're flying off." My mother more or less pushed me out of the door onto the street. Uncle Arnold waved after us for a long time. "If only the good man would go inside, for God's sake," my mother mumbled. "I can't keep this up." When he had eventually closed the door she leant against the wall of the first house we came to and laughed until the tears ran down her face. "Baron Zieyep," she moaned. "Baron Zieyep. How could you say such a terrible thing?"

"What's so terrible about it?"

After she got her breath back I was given a bowdlerised account. The old baroness's husband, a very clever businessman who had earned a lot of money, had been made a baron for services to his country. In Belgium such a person was sometimes called "Baron Zeep", Baron Soap.

"But why was she so furious about that? If he manufactured such good soap that he was made a baron, I'd be proud of the fact."

My mother was overcome once again. "Oh . . . You never understand anything." That was true. I was glad she was laughing this time and in a good mood. On the wide avenue the lighted lamps had festive veils of light rain and the trees gave off the scent of spring. In some of the windows of the houses we passed the curtains had not been closed and through one of them we saw children larking about with a cat, while in another a large and animated family was enjoying a meal. Everyone seemed to be happy, that evening, in Gabriel's city . . . And tomorrow I would have to go away again. Away from Lucie.

I asked whether I could just pop round to tell her I would not be coming to play the piano the next day.

"Oh, go on then," my mother said, turning grumpy. "Lucie this and Lucie that. I'm starting to feel sick to death of the woman. As far as that's concerned it's a good thing we're leaving. She monopolises you. Make sure she brings you home, and soon; it's almost dark."

On the other side of the street, Lucie was at her door, about to go in. I clutched her arm. She was startled. "Oh, it's you. What's wrong?"

"I just came round to say I can't come tomorrow. All of a sudden we're going home."

Her face darkened. "Oh, what a pity. We'll miss you and I've asked Gabriel to make you something really lovely and it's not finished yet."

"What is it Lucie, what is it?"

"Oh no, I'm not telling you. It's a secret. We'll send it to you. Write your address nice and clearly in here."

She took a purple leather-bound book out of her bag and looked dejected as I wrote in it by the light of the streetlamp. I was pleased when she said, in quiet despair, "I don't know where to start without you."

She accompanied me back to Grandmother's house in silence.

"Will you be in touch soon?"

"Yes, of course, and give everyone my best wishes, your father and Bertha, and Salvinia and Menie and Gabriel. I need his address too, so that I can write to him."

"Just send me your letter to him. I'll make sure he gets it," Lucie said, and this time I was too sad to wave as she left.

When I walked into the dining room, Fredie was braying with laughter, his head on the table, Charlie was slapping himself on the knees and my grandmother, Mother and Rosalba were guffawing as if they would never stop.

"Zil-yeb," Fredie roared. "How did you manage to think that up so quickly?"

"I don't know," my mother gasped. "Inspiration. Pure inspiration, from shock." I went out into the hallway until they had calmed down a little. The whole story annoyed me. I had other things on my mind.

At the table everyone was happy and talkative, but although the mood had been improved no end by the two barons, our travel plans remained unchanged. The next day we had to trek northwards again.

6

AS SOON AS I SPOTTED MY FATHER STANDING ON the platform I knew it would be some time before I saw Lucie again. He was cheerful. He was holding flowers for my mother and sweets for me, and at home there was new wallpaper in two of the rooms. I hoped his business affairs had taken a turn for the better in some inexplicable way. But later it transpired that he had not paid the premium on his life insurance.

On the day determined by him in advance, we were forced to acknowledge that Wally had been right.

It was a bitter ceremony. We had each to stand before him in turn. He asked questions and whispered the answers.

"Who wrote himself a document?"

"Wise Wally."

"What did it say in that document?"

"That we would be back at our own address long before

six months had passed."

"And a good thing too!"

"And a good thing too!"

"Did it come true?"

"It came true."

"Do you acknowledge that Wally was right, verbally, in writing, publicly and humbly?"

"Yes, I acknowledge it."

"Do you acknowledge your gratitude to him for his wisdom?"

All four of us refused outright.

I had worries at school. It was hard work catching up with the lessons I had missed and I moved on to the next year with bad marks and a lot of extra work, a disgrace that I took very much to heart, although to my parents it was a matter of complete indifference. There was also a new pupil in the class who pursued me with uninvited affection, a disagreeable child with mousy plaits and pale, red-rimmed eyes. One morning when I was standing daydreaming in the playground as usual, leaning on the fence, hoping to be left alone, Polinda came up to me as she so often did. She asked whether I knew where children came from and when I said I disliked children and was always glad to see the back of them she roared with laughter and slapped herself on the pimply bare knees with delight. Mili, who could not stand her, came over in response to the laughter and asked, with a cross look in her direction, what that pest of a girl had found to snigger at. Still spluttering, Polinda told her and added, "But maybe you don't know where children come from either." To my utter amazement Mili went bright red. She snapped that she knew all about it and that making such a fuss was ridiculous and then she raced across to the other side of the playground. Although I still felt no curiosity, it hurt my pride to find myself ignorant of something that Mili, two years younger, seemed to know all about. I told Polinda she could give me the answer.

She started by asking whether I had had any blood yet and my answer, that I thought I had just as much blood as anyone else, seemed again to amuse her greatly. Then she explained what would happen to me, as it did to all women. "And that's nothing," Polinda said as I began to retch. "That's when it starts to get really dangerous. Men have something extra, which is where you get babies from." When they were married, they stuck it into their wives while they slept, but it could also happen on the street if it was very crowded. For example, if you went to watch fireworks you always had to make sure you didn't have a man standing right behind you, because the dreadful thing was, you would not even notice they were using that extra thing and before you knew it, there you were with a baby. I said I didn't believe a word of it and told her to go off and pull someone else's leg, and that I wanted nothing more to do with her. She started howling that I could ask anyone whether or not she had spoken the truth. I refused to listen to her whines and ran across the playground to Mili. Klembem lowered himself to me on a thread. "You can pretend to Polinda that you don't believe a word of what she's told you," he squeaked. "But you know better. Think of all the times big people have burst into maddening laughter at something you didn't understand, and how they laughed even louder when you asked them to explain."

One look at my upset face was enough for Mili.

"That rotten girl has told you."

"Yes."

There it ended. We never talked about it again, but on the way to school and on the way home we were no longer Mrs Antonius and Mrs Nielsen. For the time being we did not feel like having husbands and children.

7

WE HAD BEEN HOME FOR MORE THAN A MONTH BY
the time Lucie's present arrived, a music bag made of calf's
leather and lined with tobacco-coloured *moiré*. In the left-
hand corner of the flap was my name, in handwriting that
looked as though it had been painted on with a brush dipped
in liquid silver. Inside I found my first letter from Lucie, which
was an even more valuable possession than the bag.

"This is a present from everyone in the house. The leather is
from me, the lining from Bertha, Salvinia and Menie, and my
father had your name applied by one of his friends who is a
famous goldsmith. It was Gabriel who put everything together
so neatly; I don't know how many hours he must have spent on
it. We hope you agree it's a beautiful bag and we also hope you'll
be coming here again soon. We all miss you every morning and
Gabriel and I on Sunday afternoons most of all. My father would
no doubt give you his heartfelt greetings if he was here. He's in

France at the moment for a short holiday.

    With best wishes from,

    Lucie, Gabriel, Salvinia Natans, Menie Oberberg, Bertha Zuil."

Every one of those who had signed the letter was sent a note of thanks, but I begged Lucie to write again soon. Like all creatures in love, I felt she should write more, and more often, although in fact she kept me up-to-date at regular intervals on all the notable events that took place in the Mardell household. Gabriel was now working for a much higher salary. He had bought a new suit and took pleasure in forbidding his mother to do any cooking or mending for other people, although secretly she still did. Bertha had been operated on for appendicitis, but now she was as good as recovered. Menie and Salvinia had firm marriage plans at last, "so in ten years from now perhaps something may come of it," Lucie wrote, the "perhaps" underlined. She ended all her letters with "Come back to us soon, I miss you", which always caused me pain in the region where I supposed my heart was to be found.

I kept the letters in a box that I had until then always thought too pretty to use. Mili and I had each been given one by her grandfather when he was in one of his rare good moods. The boxes were covered with red velvet and had mother-of-pearl snail shells all over them. In the middle of the shell garden on the lid was an unexpected growth, a rock-hard, egg-shaped red velvet protuberance. "That's the pin cushion," Grandpa Harry explained. "But only for very bold pins." On the inside of the lid, behind a sheet of glass, was a view of the pier. On the glass, in pink curlicues, it said "*Salutations affectueuses de Scheveningue*," because Grandpa Harry, who had trained in Paris, was an ardent Francophile. In the five souvenir shops of which he was the owner, scattered strategically across the resort, all messages aimed at the tourist population were expressed in his own individual version of the French language. Every sentence he spoke in his native tongue was ornamented at the very least with an "*Oh, là, là!*" or a "*Tiens, tiens!*"

He went about dressed in tails and in all seasons he wore white spats on his pointed patent-leather shoes. He never had a warm word to say for anything, with the exception of the France he had known in his youth and Mili, her mother and Mistinguett.* He loathed and despised humanity in general, the Germans and his wife, who belonged to that nation, in particular. Although she was capable and diligent in helping to run his retail empire, she could do nothing right as far

* Mistinguett (1875–1956), born Jeanne Florentine Bourgeois, was a French actress and singer, at one time the highest-earning female entertainer in the world.

as he was concerned and he invariably referred to her as "*mommaleur*". It took me some time to discover that this strange word indicated both French and German misfortune.

Since Grandpa Harry was always furious with something or someone, Mili and I were not surprised when we came home one day after school and heard him as soon as we stepped into the hall, ranting and raving.

We were just making ourselves scarce when the living-room door opened and Aunt Eva came out. With tears in her eyes and trembling lips she said we must not go upstairs because we first had to help her to calm her father, who was terribly upset.

Mili and I looked at each other, knowing she was talking nonsense. Grandpa Harry was impossible to calm when something really got his goat, least of all by us, but Aunt Eva was too mild-mannered to admit that she wanted us to share in the fun. Mili asked with a sigh what the matter was this time.

"Nothing's the matter at all, really," her mother giggled. "Uncle Bobby is coming back." Uncle Bobby, she told me, was her youngest brother. He had been a very black sheep for a while, "the poor boy", and although he seemed to have turned his life around, his father still wanted nothing to do with him. He was angrier than ever because it now tran-spired that "*mommaleur*", in secret and against his orders, had always kept in touch with the scoundrel.

Grandpa Harry failed to notice that his daughter had left the room and our arrival also escaped his attention. He lay on the divan hissing and squirming like an adder, caught up in a dialogue with himself that he kept repeating word for word.

It was marvellous.

"His lordship simply has to go to Turkey for cigarettes . . ."

"Papa will pay . . ."

"His lordship returns. Without cigarettes, without money, but with a fez on his arse."

"Papa will pay . . ."

"His lordship has to go to America . . ."

"Papa must forgive and forget everything because his lordship comes back with a great thimble-and-twill Jewess."

Grandpa Harry was a Jewish anti-Semite. Such a thing was not uncommon among our contemporaries. They took a relatively innocent pleasure in it of a kind no longer available to the gas-chamber generation.

Mili and I went to stand near the divan to be sure of not missing anything. We were too stunned to find it funny, but every time the balancing of the fez was mentioned we pinched each other's arms with pure delight. All good things come to an end, however. Grandpa Harry grew short of breath. He rattled off his lines one last time, rather more slowly and with longer pauses, up to and including "His lordship has to go to America . . ." and then he could get no further. He flopped backwards, ashen, eyes closed. Aunt Eva cooed "and he comes back with a skyscraper on his you-know-what" and that was too much for Mili and me. We rolled on the floor, sick with laughter.

After a while Grandpa Harry sat up and asked in astonishment what it was we found so funny. Then he requested a cup of coffee, quietly drank it, and chatted with us, very amiable by his standards, about one thing or another and about Mistinguett. He seemed a little embarrassed at his own strange behaviour. Only as he was leaving did he return to the subject of his lost son's homecoming.

"You can do or say whatever you like, Eva," he said, his hand on the door knob. "I don't want anything to do with that *mauvais garnement*." When he had pulled the door shut behind him, Aunt Eva pointed out with joy that he had spoken French and everything was alright again. We had helped her enormously, she said.

The black sheep was sensible enough to pay all his debts before his return. When he arrived in a lily-white car, Grandpa Harry gave him an emotional hug and "*mom-maleur*" was happy for the first time in years.

For Mili and her mother an exciting time of parties and outings began. Aunt Thimble-and-Twill (Mili called her Twill for short and I never did get to hear her real name) was one of those shrieking women who feel unhappy unless surrounded by people. In the twinkling of an eye she succeeded in becoming the noisy centre of all her in-laws and a large circle of brand-new friends.

The only one who did not join in the general fraternisation was Uncle Wally. He grew more sombre by the day and came to seek refuge with us whenever his wife and daughter were yet again out on the town.

"The world is the staircase," he said darkly.

He told of a naughty girl who, when at last she came back to the tiny upstairs apartment where her mother lived, was received by her with the angry words, "The whole world is outraged by it". The transgressor replied, not the least bit contrite, "Ah, Mother, the world is the staircase."

"True enough," Uncle Wally went on. "Everyone has their own staircase and that damnable Bobby, now raising hell in my family, knew no peace until he could show off his wealth in the city where he lived as a boy." My father said that all the same it was nice for the family that things were going so well for Bobby now. Uncle Wally shook his head. "I can do nothing about it," he said. "But all the same I see the phoney-bono sticking out a mile."

I heard from Mili that he had been having a document delivered to himself daily, which did a good deal to spoil the fun she and her mother were having.

Had I not longed for Lucie all the time, I would have enjoyed my summer holiday, although I saw far less than usual of Mili, who was leading a life of merriment.

The concern of contemporary parents as to how their offspring spend their free time did not trouble mine. My entertainment consisted of visiting the Mauritshuis Museum or the zoo every Sunday afternoon with my father. Our rainy climate meant it was more often the turn of the Mauritshuis. We knew all the attendants by name and they treated us with the respect due to dedicated art connoisseurs.

The zoo in The Hague distinguished itself favourably from others by accommodating no animals in cages, aside from a few dusty monkeys, a fox and a bear. As a whole it made rather a neglected impression, but in its well-maintained hothouses we passed many a contented hour.

Aside from that, I would have preferred to spend all day playing the piano, but I had to finish my schoolwork and I needed to take account of the downstairs neighbours, who must often have cursed me. I was not allowed to go to the cinema, because my mother was convinced it represented a threat to the eyesight of the young, and she allowed swimming in the sea only when the country was tormented by a heat wave. The idea that I led a boring life never occurred to me at the time.

I no longer went to the island. I was too busy saving Lucie from burning houses or being her bridesmaid when she married the Prince of Wales, who was still a bachelor then and the only eligible match for her. Since he had royal blood, it did not matter that he was a *goy*; the Book of Esther was clear on that point.

As luck would have it all was sweetness and light between my parents, and I had given up hope of a visit to Antwerp when help arrived from an unexpected quarter.

Bobby and Twill had gone to Ostend for a week with selected courtiers and they invited Aunt Eva and Mili to join them for a day. The chauffeur with the creamy white Spijker was to fetch them and bring them home. Aunt Eva thought it a shame that two seats in that glorious vehicle would be un-occupied and told us we must not pass up this splendid opportunity of a free ride to see our family.

It became a royal procession. The inside of the car was a nest lined with lilac-coloured velvet. It was hung with vases of red carnations, and Aunt Eva had brought a picnic basket full of cold chicken and tartlets. "You never know," she said. "With punctures and so forth it's always safer to take some-thing to eat with you."

There had been no time to give notice of our invasion and we arrived at the most inconvenient moment for Grand-mother. That evening a Zionist meeting was to be held at her house and when we came in Rosalba was rushing about with the maids to put chairs in a row, while Grandmother decorated the rooms with blue and white flowers, the colours of the movement. She held Herzl, the founder of Zionism, in high regard; his portrait hung next to that of my grandfather. Because he too had sported a black beard and because he had done his best when the photograph was taken to look as much as possible like the great leader, for ages I took them to be brothers.

"Oh, heavens," Grandmother said. "This time you really can't stay here. Tonight's speaker will be lodging with us." My mother imparted to her the glad tidings that we would be gone again by evening and I crept out of the house to see Lucie.

She was not at home. Klembem had told me in advance that she would be out. Her father, Menie, Salvinia and Bertha were there. Gabriel had gone to Brussels, to the stock exchange, Mr Mardell said. He understood my disappointment. Lucie was with a friend in Bruges and would not be home until late. If I had alerted her in time, she would no doubt have postponed her outing. Before I knew it, I had told him all about Bobby and Grandpa Harry, and even about Uncle Wally's documents.

Mr Mardell was a good listener.

*

In the afternoon the aunts, too, were less than delighted to see us. At Aunt Sonja's I was sent out into the garden and when I got back indoors she was sitting sobbing while my mother stroked her head and made little consoling noises. Uncle Isi was still treading the path of wickedness.

We experienced the start of the Zionist evening after all, since Bobby and Twill could scarcely bring themselves to part from Mili and her mother, so we were picked up far later than had been arranged. I found a spot from which I could spy on Lucie's house. She failed to return before we left.

On the way home there was no time to be sad because Aunt Eva, along with Mili, had so much to tell us about the gaming rooms, where they had won twenty francs, and about Twill, who had lost a valuable pearl necklace the previous night, although that did not trouble her in the least since she had five of them, each more beautiful than the last.

"I'm sure it must be wonderful to be so rich," Aunt Eva said. "And she's so generous, nothing is too much to ask. She would love to meet all of you sometime."

We said nothing. Out of solidarity with Wally, my father had forbidden us to have anything to do with that particular lady. "A piece of riffraff," he called her, and when he said that about someone it was his last word on the matter.

A few days later I received a letter from Lucie in which, in the most flattering terms, she expressed regret at having missed my unannounced visit. Grandmother wrote that she had found it a pity to have so little time for us and she invited us to come and stay for her birthday at the end of August. To save myself further disappointment I wrote to Lucie without delay to ask whether she was thinking of taking a holiday at precisely that time and her answer was reassuring: she preferred to travel in winter and was already looking forward to our long walks.

Now I somehow had to get through ten days of July and three weeks of August, and there was no-one with whom I could talk about Lucie. My mother was set against the entire friendship and Mili thought it odd that I could so much like such an old person.

"But you like your aunt, don't you?"

An aunt was an aunt, Mili said. That was not the same as a friend. No, she still thought it odd. I could talk to my father about Mr Mardell, although that meant going over old ground, since he could say little more about the man than that he was appreciative of art and had shown impeccable taste even back in the time when he had been more or less a friend, years ago.

The summer days crept by until at last we set off on our travels. On Grandmother's birthday, which brought all her children and grandchildren together in the parental home once more, there was non-stop talking, laughing and eating.

Alcoholic drinks played no part in the festivities, but there were rivers of coffee.

I was generally considered mean and heartless for wanting to visit a friend on the family's great day, but I was allowed half an hour off. I telephoned Lucie and when, close to tears, I told her how short my visit to her would be, she comforted me by saying that we could discuss a great deal in that time. I asked when I should come and to my amazement she told me to wait at our walking corner at half past three, because it would be impossible for her to receive me at home this time on account of a big secret about which her father must know nothing.

She had cut off her hair.

"Oh, Lucie, will your father be very angry?"

"Of course not, silly, I've worn it like this for ages. He likes the way it looks as a matter of fact. What do you think of it?"

"You've had it permed."

She had also had it bleached. Straw-yellow curls framed her face, which itself looked strange because she was wearing heavy make-up. She was no longer my Lucie. "I liked it better before."

She roared with laughter. "You're too conservative for your years. Just look who's here."

She sounded different; even her laugh was different.

Then a pair of hands covered my eyes. When I freed myself from them and looked round I saw Gabriel.

On top of everything.

Gabriel was pleasant enough and he could tell wonderful stories about Antwerp, but I found it a bit much to have to share with him my precious half-hour with Lucie. I greeted him stiffly.

He no longer looked like the Angel Gabriel.

He had grown broader, he was wearing a smart light-grey suit, and his hair had been pomaded. It looked neater that way, but far more ordinary. On his finger was a gold signet ring with a green stone that had a large G engraved in it. Even his voice had changed.

It was all a bit unnerving. Half an hour turned out to be a very long time.

"Aren't you curious?" asked Lucie. "Can't you guess what it is?"

No, I could not. Lucie thrust her arm through Gabriel's. "She's someone who ought to know, don't you think?"

He nodded. "She made a big enough contribution."

"Well then," Lucie said. "Here we go. Gabriel and I have loved each other for a very long time and we are engaged, but that fact needs to be withheld for now, even from my father and Gabriel's mother."

If she had hit me on the head with a hammer I could

not have been more stunned. Her eyes and her half-open mouth gleamed moistly. The inside of her lower lip looked sickly pale against the cyclamen colour of the lashings of lipstick she had applied.

Proud, self-assured Lucie . . . She looked so helpless, even a little stupid.

It was alarming and incomprehensible.

"Won't you even congratulate us?" The purple mouth smiled. I shook their proffered hands and mumbled something that I hoped was appropriate.

"If you're my good friend, then you mustn't be jealous," Lucie declared. Indignant, I told her I was not jealous, only surprised. Gabriel claimed he understood well enough why I would be; he could not think what she saw in him. I asked why their engagement had to be kept a secret from Mr Mardell, who loved Gabriel so much.

"For that very reason," Lucie said, with a familiar angry cast to her lips, and Gabriel explained that because Lucie's father had placed so much trust in him, he felt obliged to demonstrate what he was worth before asking for his daughter's hand.

Then they started praising me to the skies. If I had not been with them on those Sunday afternoon walks, they would never have got to know each other better. They were so grateful to me; they would always regard me as their good fairy, their very best friend . . .

Why must Gabriel's mother not know of it?

Because she was incapable of keeping her mouth shut. If she knew, then by the next day the whole of Pelikaanstraat would have got to hear about it, Gabriel said, and he asked whether it would be hard for me to keep their secret. No, they could rest assured, I would not betray them to anyone. In our excitement we had been walking at quite a pace and I was startled to discover that we had almost reached the end of the Meir and I could not possibly be back by four. Gabriel suggested visiting a small chapel where Joanna the Mad had not been married – it was nearby and I was late anyhow. Lucie refused. She had no wish to look at a place where someone had not been married; it might bring her bad luck if she went there now.

"Joanna did in fact get married," Gabriel lectured. "But not in the enchanting little chapel that was prepared for her, and as it turned out it would actually have been far better for her if she had forgone the marriage altogether."

"There. See!" Lucie said. "I definitely don't want to go."

"Who's talking nonsense now?" Gabriel said.

"I am," Lucie said. "For the first time in my life, thank God."

They forgot that I was walking beside them until we were back at our point of departure.

It was arranged that Gabriel would go on ahead and Lucie would arrive home ten minutes later.

"Are you coming to play the piano tomorrow? My father would find it ill-mannered of you if you were to be in town without calling on him."

I lied, saying that I did not know whether we would still be there the next day. "I'll come and see," Lucie said. "And if you're still here you must visit." She offered to go in with me and take the blame for my late return, but I assured her I could manage on my own.

"Be a little bit happy for me," she begged. "I don't have as easy a life as you might think." I promised her that no-one in the world could be more pleased by her happiness than I was. It did not sound very convincing.

In the house I found a sad bouquet of nephews and nieces in party clothes on the staircase. They warned me not to go up, because I would only be sent away again, as they had been, with express instructions to be quiet as mice.

"The Individual" had come with Uncle Isi and everyone was furious. I had heard so much about The Individual that I wanted to see her with my own eyes for once, but I was not about to say that to the little ones. Hypocrite that I was, I claimed that I believed it was my duty to go upstairs because people might be feeling uneasy as a result of my long absence.

A deathly silence reigned in the crowded room. The dressing-down I was expecting did not occur and by gesturing feebly with one hand, Grandmother indicated that I could take a seat.

She and her relatives, along with Grandma Hofer and Rosalba, had formed a large circle around the walls of the room. They sat wordlessly staring ahead.

None of them ate a morsel or drank a drop. Uncle Isi had had the unthinkable gall to send his wife and children to the birthday party and then appear himself later in the company of the woman of his heart. Nothing like it had ever happened among us before and the rogue seemed to be enjoying the consternation.

"A person must feed himself," he said, loading a plate with delicacies that he started to nibble with a joyful grin. The uninvited guest won my sympathy straight away by saying in mocking tones to him that he must not keep speaking about himself as "a person".

"If you continue to do that we'll start to wonder whether you are a person at all; perhaps in reality you're only a beautiful animal," she said.

An audible shiver of horror ran through the ranks.

Having no other choice, since there were no chairs free along the walls, I sat in the middle of the room with the evildoers. The Individual was small and slight and had golden blonde hair. I determined that she was far less beautiful than Aunt Sonja, who always, and at that moment more than ever, looked like a pretty, sad madonna. The blonde had the face of a witty urchin, with a snub nose and huge light-blue eyes framed by long lashes. Those were false, stuck onto her eyelids with strips of paper, but they suited her tremendously well. She chattered away to me nineteen to the dozen in an artificially high, childlike voice. I reaped cross and reproachful glances from my blood relatives by laughing out loud when she told me that her kitchen maid had said she was going to place the complot at the centre of the table where it would have the greatest defect.

Uncle Isi stared at her, enraptured, although she did all sorts of things that he forbad his wife. She smoked one cigarette after the other, she powdered her nose and retouched her lips every few minutes, and she made all kinds of comments on Uncle Isi's manners. She told him, among other things, that he might have brought her, too, a plate of delicacies.

"But you never eat anything for fear of getting fat," he excused himself anxiously. She moped, saying a gentleman would at least have offered, and Uncle Isi, who terrorised his family, lowered his bulging, impudent dark eyes and blushed like a child. After a while, Grandma Hofer, who was sitting snorting to herself, could stand it no longer. She noisily got to her feet and declared she was leaving. She asked all those present to follow her and announced to my dismayed grandmother that they would be back in the evening, "when we can all sit in our own peaceful company; this is after all a family party". She walked past her son and his unlawful companion as if they were made of air, and all the others, apart from my grandmother, Rosalba and me, followed her lead.

The blonde giggled when the procession had passed, saying Isi could now take her home without needing to rush. She was having glorious fun. She thanked my grandmother for the amusing afternoon, wished her many happy returns, and disappeared, still giggling, in a cloud of perfume, with her admirer at her heels.

"All doors and windows wide open," Grandmother ordered. "I can't bear that stench." Then her indignation burst loose. I was scolded for having laughed at the feeble joke. Even Rosalba, who always stuck up for me, said I had disgraced myself. Grandmother bewailed her ruined birthday. Rosalba said all men were pigs and Uncle Isi the biggest pig of them all.

Grandma Hofer was praised for her courage, although she was suspected of having enjoyed the fact that the trouble had occurred at Grandmother's party. I came close to tears when I was asked to go and fetch the two incensed women's sewing boxes from upstairs. There seemed to be no end to this no-day. First that whole story with Lucie and now this. I could not help having laughed at the inarticulate kitchen maid, could I? Grandmother's sewing box was made of ebony, its lid inlaid with flowers of mother-of-pearl. In it she kept *batiste* and the most expensive lace, from which she made her frills and handkerchiefs. The never-shrinking supply of socks for Rosalba to darn was packed away in a cardboard box covered with floral-print paper, which she had been given as a present, filled with sweets, on one of her birthdays.

Grandmother, in her most elegant silk gowns, and Rosalba, as ever in a white blouse and a narrow black skirt that reached to her shoes, sat facing each other at a window and as soon as they saw the familiar boxes their ill-feeling evaporated. They put on their glasses, visibly pleased to be able to get cracking again as normal.

I noticed that I was hungry and asked whether I might take some of the almost untouched delicacies.

"A person must feed himself," Grandmother said, and she began to laugh so merrily that she had to put down her sewing.

The truth came to light. They confessed that they had struggled to stop themselves from bursting out laughing during the visit by Isi and that comical creature. Because comical she was, as Rosalba, who had not even been able to

134

understand everything she said, was forced to admit. And elegant! That sand-coloured suit could not have cost a cent under five hundred guilders, and of course Isi had paid, you had better believe it. Sonja was far more beautiful and an excellent wife and mother, yet my grandmother, or so she claimed, was objective enough to understand that her husband must sometimes be bored by her eternal goodness. Things had got altogether out of hand. Although Grandmother and Rosalba competed in praising her good qualities at the start of every sentence, Aunt Sonja's shortcomings were scrutinised at length. Having justified their *schadenfreude*, they kept going over the course of events from beginning to end until they fell into a satisfied sleep. I was sitting next to Rosalba on a high stool, a skein of wool around my arms. The ball she was winding still in her hand, she sat with her head on her flat breast, snoring. Rosalba's snore consisted of a thin whistle that seemed to come out of her nose, and at the same time her lips produced a bubbling noise.

Grandmother, less of a virtuoso, merely deepened her breathing and gave a soft moan from time to time. I had learned that few misdeeds are counted against a person to such a degree on earth or in the afterlife as the disturbing of elderly people in their sleep. I carefully let the wool slide onto my lap, but apart from that I did not dare to move a muscle.

Across from the house was a pharmacy, on the corner of a side street. In the window that graced our avenue were two giant glass flagons, one filled with an orange liquid, the other blue-green. They caught the sunlight in their colourful bellies and I stared at them until I saw rainbows when I shut my eyes. After that there was little left to look at, apart from the portrait of my grandfather hanging on the wall behind Grandmother's chair. He died before I was born and there was nothing left of him, aside from a few sarcastic remarks that lived on among us like oracular sayings, and the straight narrow nose his offspring prided themselves on if they were fortunate enough to resemble him. My feet went to sleep, but the rest of me remained stubbornly awake. I was just about to hazard an escape attempt when I noticed that the two women were no longer snoring. My grandmother was sitting lopsided in her armchair, mouth wide open. Rosalba, floppy as a puppet, was leaning against the window. They were pale as corpses – they were dead, and everyone would suspect me of having killed them silently if I failed to go and fetch help. On the other hand, if I left the corpses, even for a moment, that too would count against me.

It was indeed sad that my poor granny had to die on her birthday and I found it touching that her faithful maid did not abandon her even in death, but I would be blamed for it and end up in prison. Or might I, as a minor, be sent to reform school?

What a disgrace it must be to have a daughter who had murdered two women at the tender age of twelve and such good creatures too, women who had never treated her with anything but friendliness. I was feeling sorry for my parents to the point of distraction, more so than for my victims, when Fredie and Charlie came in singing loudly to wish Grandmother a happy birthday.

Grandmother and Rosalba rose from the dead and to Fredie's teasing question as to whether they had slept well they both said they had not shut their eyes for a moment, they had been sewing, all afternoon they had been sewing, had they not, Gittel?

With two unsolved murders on my conscience I confirmed the fact with a straight face.

"This better?" Lucie said on the way to the other side of the street the next morning. She had her own sweet face again and her curls were far less lavish.

"Much better."

She said I was a bossy creature and reminded me of my oath of loyalty. There was no need for that. It had disturbed my sleep.

Mr Mardell thought I did not look well. "Too many sweets

yesterday?" That too, and it had been such a troublesome day.

Did I have anything to tell him that I thought was funny, like the last time about that gentleman who wrote letters to himself?

How could he think I found that dismal tomfoolery funny? I needn't be embarrassed to admit it, Mr Mardell said. There was far more to be gained by drawing the comical element out of a less-than-pleasant experience than by trying to track down some non-existent sunny side to it, as was usually recommended by people who ought to know better. I had no desire to contradict him, even though I could not have disagreed more. Off the cuff I could have come up with a whole series of experiences that were not to be laughed at: going to school; Aron's death; the taunts of the family about my father's precarious business ventures; Lucie's engagement . . .

Instead I supplied him with a faithful account of Uncle Isi's misdeeds, and I had just been rewarded with brief applause for my rendition of Grandma Hofer's "I'm leaving and I would ask all those present to follow me" when Lucie came in to report that my mother had telephoned to tell her to bring me back at once, since as a result of unforeseen circumstances we were to depart on the next train for Holland.

Mr Mardell insisted I ring to ask the cause of this hasty

retreat. He thought my father must be ill. I suspected a difference of opinion with someone or other. We were both wrong.

That evening a big party was to be held at Uncle Wally's house and in a telegram he had requested the presence of my mother. "That is at least a pleasant reason," Mr Mardell said. "What a relief!"

"It's always so quiet here."

"Yes, you must find that rather boring sometimes." I had to search for appropriate words to give him to understand that it was the peace that I found so pleasant. Mili was right – it was hard to be friends with old people. Whatever you said, they only half understood, if at all. "Shouldn't she say hello to Gabriel, now that she's leaving us so soon?"

"No, Father," Lucie said. "She really does have to go right away or her mother will be very angry." My whole face turned red, and it went even redder when I saw that Mr Mardell was looking at me with amusement and even a hint of pity.

"I believe she would like to see him for a moment."

"Oh no, oh no . . ." I started to sweat.

"What's wrong with you all of a sudden?" Lucie said, annoyed.

"I really do have to leave." I shook their hands as fast as I could and raced out of the room.

Mr Mardell thought I had fallen for Gabriel.

On our arrival home it turned out that Wally had made peace with his brother-in-law.

"*Pack schlägt sich und verträgt sich,*" my father said: rabble are quick to put their differences aside. It took some effort to persuade him to attend the feast of reconciliation, but the next morning at breakfast he said he had found Bobby far nicer than he expected. They had engaged in a very sensible conversation about opportunities for doing business with America, but that woman was and always would be a piece of riffraff, impossible to treat like a respectable person.

The end of the holiday was in sight when we received news of the death of Baroness Bommens. "Rejoicing she now stands before the throne of God," her death notice assured us. She would no doubt rejoice a good deal louder when she saw the baron again.

My father wrote a sensitive letter to the relatives and the reply from "our Bommens" led us to conclude that the house with all its contents was to be sold. Lucien and Robert would be sent to a boarding school and Madame Odette had already been working for some days in his bar.

The next time we went to stay with Grandmother we would have to look for an alternative place of refuge.

"A door is being shut for ever," I muttered to myself. "By the cold Hand of Death." I found that so beautifully sad and stirringly formulated that I burst into tears. My astonished mother said she had never realised I cared so much about the old lady.

The baroness' passing made such a deep impression on me that I was even able to feel a little sympathy for Lucien and Robert – they would have a tough time of it at that boarding school. Madame Odette, who after a lifetime of luxury would now have to work hard to support herself, I pitied with all my heart.

I spent the last few days of the holiday in mourning.

"Being grown up brings a good deal of misery with it, but at least you don't have to go to school," I said to Mili as we undertook our daily walk to that hated building again for the first time. Mili did not agree. She liked going to school, and becoming an adult seemed an attractive prospect to her. You could stay up as late as you pleased and drive a car and go to parties whenever you felt like it. I did not contradict her, although I knew better. Being an adult meant telling lies, spreading slander, worrying about money and having stomach ache. For several months I had been troubled by a particularly unpleasant kind of pain in the lower stomach. My mother said there was nothing to be done about it. It was caused by nature, because soon I would be an adult woman. It was a blue pain. I failed to understand how all the women I knew could go about with smiles on their faces if they were having to suffer it time and again. I could only assume you got used to it eventually.

Mili asked how my friend in Antwerp was doing and I said it was a secret that I was not allowed to talk about.

"Don't, then." She shrugged. "I'll see you around." She raced over to one of her classmates.

At twelve o'clock she walked home a few paces ahead of me, laughing exasperatingly and whispering with two girls. I regretted my remark. It had been unkind of me, and boastful, to talk about my secret. Stupid, too. Imagine if she spoke about it at home and in some indirect way Mr Mardell got to hear of it.

The two other children turned into a side street and Mili walked on alone, whistling bravely. I caught up with her.

"Don't be angry. I was being silly."

"Yes, you were, and not such a little bit either."

"Are we friends again now?"

"Ye-es," Mili said. "And anyway she's a cow." There would no doubt have been some more bitter words to follow had we not seen Uncle Wally and Aunt Eva going into my parents' house just at that moment.

"They must be coming to fetch me," Mili said. "Bit strange, when we live so close."

"Something bad has probably happened."

This time I was right. Pale as death, the four parents were standing in the cramped little room we called our salon.

"They've gone," Aunt Eva said, her voice hoarse.

Bobby and Twill had vanished without trace. No further information was forthcoming.

Aunt Eva handed out bars of chocolate with a melancholy smile and then Mili and I were sent away. In my little bedroom, which barely had space for us both, Mili went to stand at the window with her back to me. "Uncle Bobby was a nice man," she said. "And I don't want to hear a bad word about him." At that she muttered in a quivering voice the verse from which she always took comfort when she needed it.

> At ten you're only small.
> At twenty, love is all,
> At thirty, wedding bells,
> At forty your age tells.
> At fifty you're infirm,
> At sixty past your term,
> At seventy going down,
> At eighty in the ground.
> Ninety you might just get to be,
> But a hundred you'll probably never see.

8

THE MARK PLUMMETED AND A FEW DAYS LATER
uncle Wally came to tell us he had decided to go and live in
Germany. He resolutely sold off all he owned and before
we fully realised what was happening, he and his family
had gone. Mili's nanny was left behind in the Netherlands,
crushed. She took a job as a shop assistant in a small drapery
shop. "I'll never get used to another family," she snivelled.
She took to visiting us whenever she had a free afternoon.
Whereas previously she had paid me little if any attention,
she was now embarrassingly humble in her efforts to curry
favour. On every visit she brought some dismal present or
other with her, a useful object from the shop where she was
working with such reluctance, a darning mushroom, pins, or
a card of press studs, for which it took me a major effort to
muster joyful thanks. In my mother's view, moreover, those
things must surely have been pilfered, and she expressed the

hope that the police never found out or I would be arrested for receiving stolen goods. Even on her better days, nanny had always been an unattractive bag of bones. Now, with chronically tearful eyes and a fiery nose, she looked very much like a scarecrow. All the photographs ever taken of Mili bulged out of her worn handbag and whenever a letter arrived she would read it out to us more than once, sobbing.

The postcards Mili sent me from time to time were gazed upon by nanny with such an envious, avaricious look that I handed them over to her. My experience with Lucie had taught me what it meant to yearn for a message from someone you loved. Since Lucie's engagement my adoration of her had cooled, and in any case I had little time left to be sad after new neighbours moved in downstairs. The previous tenants had been driven away by Czerny and Clementi and with the new ones, a youthful, gadabout journalist couple, I had been able to reach a good arrangement; they made me promise not to play while they were compiling reports for their newspaper, but other than that I could carry on as much as I liked.

I had piano lessons once a week. My teacher was so old he had played for King William III. On that occasion the monarch gave him a gold watch which he still carried with him. When he was satisfied with my progress I was allowed to examine it, which I did with great respect, although there was little to admire about it.

Meanwhile the consequences of my father's way of doing business were more and more disastrous. Heart-rending sighs could be heard in the evenings as he worked on his stamp collection. Banning Cocq and Uncle Salomon took the stage more and more often and my mother made plans to move to Antwerp with me for good. This time I did not know whether to be happy at the prospect; nor did I know whether I would dare to visit Lucie. The decision was taken out of my hands.

Nanny came storming in on an afternoon when we were not expecting her, holding a large bunch of ribbons in either hand, in various colours.

She stopped in the middle of the room and shouted that her freedom had been bought. From the confused cries that followed we were able to make out that Uncle Wally had appeared at the draper's shop as her avenging angel. To nanny's delight he had accused the proprietors, who had not treated her at all badly, of being bloodsuckers and parasites. "This was a blossoming young woman when I left her here. What is she now? A living skeleton!" he had shouted, and after throwing the equivalent of three months' salary down at their feet he took nanny to a restaurant where, or so she said, she wanted to eat everything she had been forced to go without for the past six months. By mistake she kept hold of the ribbons she was putting into the window display at the moment he arrived (my mother gave me a meaningful look) and because she never wanted to set foot over the threshold of that wretched place again, they were to be given to Mili.

After dinner Uncle Wally needed to speak with important business contacts and nanny had been sent to us as his envoy to announce his visit that same evening.

The next morning she was to leave with him for Berlin "first class reserved" and he had forbidden her to spend her last night in her boarding house, instead insisting that she must stay at the expensive hotel where he had taken a room.

She was drunk with euphoria.

Before she left she offered me one of the ribbons, and when I declined, polite but firm, she said, "Ah, yes, I see that you're right. Those pastel colours don't suit you. You'd have done far better to be born a boy, with that strange broad face of yours."

Tense, we awaited Uncle Wally's arrival.

When he appeared late in the evening he looked impressive, just the way I had always imagined a captain of industry. A large collar of astrakhan fur adorned his brand-new navy-blue winter coat, a pale-grey castor hat his angular head, a fat gold knob his very yellow walking stick.

"I don't have much time," he began, after a hasty greeting. "But never let it be said of Wally that he abandoned his old friends to their misery. No, no, don't contradict me. You are living in misery, I can see that at a glance." He turned to me. "Just you tell your uncle Wally: aren't you going to Antwerp with your mother soon?"

"Yes, Uncle Wally. The day after tomorrow."

"See!" he said in triumph. "I knew it."

Meanwhile he had removed his glorious outer layer and was now presenting himself in all the splendour of a camel-coloured suit and red silk shirt. After deigning to drink tea with us, he said, "And now you must listen."

He spoke long and loud but my father was not convinced. "I am dogged by misfortune," he mumbled. "I've come to realise that there's no point in trying to escape my fate."

"Yes, yes," Wally said. "If you'd become a baker no-one would be allowed to eat bread any longer, I've heard that from you so often, but now the time has come to break the vicious circle. Just think how wonderful it will be for Gittel to be able to study music in Berlin."

I was sent to bed and the next morning my mother told me that after careful consideration it had been decided that we too would go to Germany. Our visit to Antwerp had been cancelled.

Busy weeks followed. I said an emotional goodbye to my friendly old music teacher and the only thing that reconciled me to the wild plan was the prospect of seeing Mili again. The last few days in our stripped rooms were at least exciting, as was my first long international train journey, but my mother was the only one of us to enjoy herself without restraint. She always felt happy as soon as she smelled a railway station.

Our train was met in Berlin by Mili and her parents.

"We've rented a raffinous flat for you," Wally told us. "And so cheap, five million a week."

We had yet to grow accustomed to those astronomical numbers, but the place he took us to was indeed a very attractive dwelling. We were welcomed by the owners, an elderly lady and her son, Helmut. They now lived in just two rooms of the luxurious flat and were pleased to have a family of "*steinreicher Holländer*" as tenants. Persian carpets had been laid wherever there was space for them and all the rooms were crammed full of brand-new lemonwood furniture. Helmut soon confided in us that he had so little confidence in the markets that he had decided it was wiser to invest his entire capital in goods.

Mili and I greeted each other with meticulously feigned indifference and only when we found ourselves amid the lemonwood in my large, elegant bedroom did she say with un-familiar stiffness, "It's nice that you're here, although now you've got a better-looking home than we have." She helped me to hang up my sailor suits, which looked lost in the more than life-sized mirrored wardrobe.

When we went downstairs, Helmut introduced us to his

149

fiancée, a pale, reticent creature who waited on him and her future mother-in-law hand and foot.

"But I'll never marry her," he said after she disappeared into the kitchen again. All in all it was a confusing evening and I was glad when at last I was lying in bed.

The next morning my father left early to see Uncle Wally, who had promised to introduce him to some powerful businessmen.

I would be going to school with Mili just like in the old days and Aunt Eva had even sought out a music teacher for me and made an appointment for the afternoon of our first full day in Berlin.

Mili's mother hugged me when she gave me this piece of good news, saying she was convinced I would feel properly at home in Berlin only when I knew that I would be having good piano lessons again.

The teacher's name was Knieper and according to the information Aunt Eva had been given about her she had once been a famous concert pianist herself and now had an excellent reputation as a teacher. I was able to look forward to meeting Mrs Knieper without qualms, since my teacher in The Hague had been wise enough to impress upon me when we parted that I must above all do my best for his successors as I had done for him.

All four of us went.

She lived not far from Mili, on the ground floor of a similar apartment block. We were admitted by a thin boy with a narrow mousy face, his wet hair smoothly combed back. He greeted each of us with a deep bow. Then he took us to a small hallway with wooden, rush-bottomed chairs. He asked us to take our seats and to be patient for a little while, as his mother was still busy giving a lesson.

He gestured towards a wooden door in a pointed arch, with copper nails that spelled out in Gothic letters "Music Room" and underneath "Silence!" Beyond the door, Schumann's "*Aufschwung*" was being appallingly abused.

The boy asked us to excuse him, since he had homework to do, and before he crept away he gave the four of us another bow. He forgot to turn on the light and in the dark hallway we were treated to the first eight bars of "*Aufschwung*", repeated over and over with the same mistakes every time. Suddenly it was played differently, complete with the mistakes but with a masterful touch, while an angry voice sang "This night I saw Fanny walking / In a pair of red pyjamas.":

The playing stopped and after a brief, fierce exchange of words that to our regret we were unable to follow, the door opened and a young girl with a music bag clamped under her arm shot past us, sobbing, brushing our knees as she went. The door was slammed shut behind her. Aunt Eva said with a laugh that she had swallowed a big chunk of her fur collar with shock and Mili put all her fingers into her mouth to keep herself from snorting with laughter. My mother greatly enjoyed the incident as well, but I knew that to the end of my days I would hear those words, that odd couplet, in the middle of the main theme of "*Aufschwung*" – and it was one of my favourite pieces.

Some time passed before the door opened again and a robust woman emerged.

"Follow me," she said.

Obeying her cool command, we walked behind her into a long room of which two grand pianos, because of their unusual arrangement with the keyboards side by side, took up almost the entire width. There was also a divan covered with a dark-brown tarpaulin. Below and on top of the pianos were piles of music, and racks had been built against one of the walls, filled with books in identical black-and-gold bindings that gave the impression of having been bought by the metre.

In a trembling voice, in which her bout of laughter

continued to reverberate, Aunt Eva introduced us to Mrs Knieper, who looked like a lioness with a cold.

She was wearing a pseudo-Greek gown of grey flannel. She said she was not in the habit of receiving aspiring pupils who arrived accompanied by a regiment. In my case she was willing to make an exception because I came from the countryside and did not know the way. With a couple of gestures in the direction of the divan she gave us to understand that the regiment could station itself there but must not interfere with the further course of events.

She went to sit at one of the pianos, beckoned me over and studied me from top to toe.

"So," she scoffed. "Here we have the child prodigy."

"Oh no, madam, I'm not a child prodigy at all," I said, startled. My old teacher had instilled in me a healthy abhorrence of those unfortunate creatures. By chance I had supplied the only correct answer. "Sometimes children can be more sensible than so-called grownups," Mrs Knieper said. She gave me a far friendlier look but shook her mane at Aunt Eva. That sweet creature had praised me to the skies on her previous visit and as a result had called down the wrath of the Knieper upon herself.

Amid the sheet music on the piano I was leaning against was a large photograph that, after the fashion of the day, showed the blurred and filmy outline of a lioness-style head.

"May I take a closer look at your photo?" I asked, and again I had scored a bull's eye.

"In-ter-est-ing" – Mrs Knieper smiled with satisfaction – "that you think it's me. Everyone thinks so, but do examine it more closely."

The threesome on the slippery divan gave me admiring looks for having succeeded in taming her in such short order. I picked up the photograph and spoilt everything immediately by saying, "Oh, no, it's Leona Frey. She doesn't look a bit like you." Through the haze of the photograph I had recognised the wise eyes and witty mouth of the famous pianist. Her wild mane fell onto her shoulders in the same way as Mrs Knieper's and she too was wearing a Greek gown.

At the bottom of the portrait Leona had written a pompous dedication to her "beloved colleague", in the spidery writing common to many celebrated women.

Mrs Knieper said with venom that Leona and she were often taken for twins and that I must now do what I had come to do, namely play for her, since she had neither the time nor the desire to hear any more idle chatter.

She listened, eyes closed, to the first two pages of Beethoven's "Rondo in C Major", waved that she had heard enough and asked which piece my teacher had proposed working through with me had I stayed in the countryside.

"Bach's 'Italian Concerto'," I said, with some pride.

In sweet tones that ought to have had the effect of a warning, Mrs Knieper asked, "Why not the 'Appassionata' straight away?" I promptly fell into the trap. "Oh, do you really think I'd be able to play it?"

She laughed a hard, bitter laugh and signalled to me to come and stand beside her.

"When a talented pianist has studied under the best masters for twenty years, and furthermore has drained every last drop from the cups of sorrow and joy, even then such a person would hesitate to play the 'Appassionata', and you, stupid child, think you could do so already."

Her muscled hands gripped my shoulders and gave me a good shaking. From her breath I could tell that before we came in she had drained every last drop from several cups, filled with brandy. She continued speaking for a full five minutes and in that short time expertly razed me to the ground.

My social circle, which had to a shameful degree spoilt and overestimated me, was subjected to several ferocious lashes as well. At last she said that she did feel there was a chance of considerably reducing, within a few years, many serious faults that marred my playing, although alas not all of them; some had become ingrained. At that point she asked for three months' fee in advance, an impressive number of millions, which my mother paid without batting an eyelid. To us a million either way was of little significance.

Mrs Knieper announced that I was to receive a lesson from her once a week at the same hour and in preparation for the first lesson I must practise three scales. For six months I would not be allowed to play anything else and before we left she wanted us to hear the sort of music that could be made by someone of my own age.

She went to the door, roared "Hänschen!", and the boy mouse came in.

"You have heard this little girl try to play Beethoven, now you do it the way it should be done," his mother commanded him. Hänschen did not hesitate for a moment. Out of the simple rondo he drew all the serene peace and loveliness it contains, and the twists and turns in the tricky passage that I always struggled with caused his nimble little fingers no trouble at all.

It cut me to pieces.

After Hänschen, with a dignified nod in recognition of our applause, had left the room, his mother gave me a penetrating look.

"Well, what do you say to that?"

Aunt Eva hastened to my aid. "Very lovely," she said.

Mrs Knieper snapped that she had been speaking to me.

With a heavy heart I was forced to acknowledge that it had been outstanding and that Hänschen could already be counted among the great pianists.

"That is at least honest," she said. "Yes, he has an extra-ordinary talent. I'll keep him with me for another year and then Leona will take him under her personal guidance. Now you can leave and I'll expect you here next week with three scales, unaccompanied."

She laughed under her breath at her own joke and with one of her expressive gestures she swept us out of the room. It was pitch dark in the little hall now, and we thumped and painfully bumped our way to the front door.

Out on the street my mother, who had heard her falcon declared to be the lowliest of owls, stared ahead in tragic silence.

Aunt Eva exhausted herself with apologies and offered to reimburse the advanced lesson-millions, since it was unthinkable that I would return to that-witch-of-a-Knieper; but I insisted on taking the lessons and pretended to be undaunted by her.

Mili said she thought Hänschen was a rotter and she had never in her life heard anyone play the piano so lousily.

A completely unjustified verdict that cheered us up no end.

My mother and I spent the week that followed the visit to the Kniepers in a flush of millions. In recent years she had been forced to watch every penny to prevent it from leaving her purse, so for her it was bliss to be able to buy anything she fancied. My father refused to participate in our spending orgies. He looked more and more downcast and said he was grateful that his parents had not experienced the shame of seeing their son, who had left his country an honest man, return as a "*Schieber*". I did not know what a *Schieber* was and I had no time or inclination to try and find out. With the help of Aunt Eva, who knew all the best places, my mother clothed herself and me in new garments from top to toe. Of course she bought me another sailor suit, but this time it was made of a fluffy scarlet fabric and its sky-blue silk collar was decorated with silver braiding: a fitting costume for a monkey on an organ.

After our predatory raids we returned in good cheer to our lemonwood paradise. In the salon stood a two-metre-long Bechstein grand, on which I diligently unleashed Knieper's scales. Sometimes Helmut's slave came to ask me to play something for her and sobbed silently in a corner as I did so. I would have loved to believe it was the moving qualities of my playing that made such a deep impression on her, but she kept telling me, unasked, of fresh misdeeds by her blonde beast. My mother comforted the unfortunate soul with bonbons or a glass of liqueur and then we were able to forget her and her sorrow amid the life of Berlin.

We drank tea *unter den Linden* and for the first time in

my life I ate at non-Jewish eating places. How my parents reconciled this with their kosher consciences was a mystery, but it was so lovely and grand in the restaurants that I was careful not to bring up such a delicate subject. During that unforgettable week I met a boy I liked for the first time, a second cousin, who had a wonderful talent for drawing. When I mentioned him to Mili she asked, matter-of-factly, whether I was in love with him. Oh no, I just thought he was nice. "That's impossible," Mili said. "You think girls are nice and with boys you fall in love."

Our attendance at an operetta-for-adults was the high-point of our glory week. Mili had been out at night in Berlin with her parents before and as she studied the programme she discussed with great expertise the various stars twinkling on the heavenly stage at that moment.

"This lot are a bit *Schmiere*," she said. I would rather have died than ask her to explain the unfamiliar word. I understood that it was contemptuous and it took a huge effort on my part to contain my admiration for everything that was happening on the stage, which was plenty.

There were singing gentlemen in cornflower-blue uniforms and there was a ravishing blonde lady who stepped out of the frame of a painting in a bedroom where it was obvious she did not belong. There she sang, very movingly, along with a gentleman who was wearing a most beautiful uniform, with gold tassels all over it, and then the lights went out. A short time later the lights came up again and in the frame was a perfectly ordinary painting. The beautiful lady had gone for good and had I not wanted to keep up appearances in front of Mili I would have been moved to tears. After the performance was over we went for supper in a restaurant decorated in Spanish style. We were served by blonde toreadors. A Spanish pair performed a tango on a stage not much bigger than a tablecloth. Their black eyes shone, their white teeth flashed, the castanets clattered, the señorita's colourful skirts flapped, the agile feet of the dancers stamped a drum roll on the floor, and I gave my tears free rein.

"*Beschwipst,*" Mili said. "She still needs to get used to life in a metropolis."

I had barely sipped at my glass of white wine, but so much bliss so suddenly was impossible to assimilate.

At the end of the week someone, a certain Dr Hjalmar Schacht, did something with the mark that meant we were just as poor as we had been at home.

My father said he was not surprised by the monetary reform, on the contrary, he was convinced that Dr Schacht had waited for him to arrive before putting it into effect.

When the rent on our apartment was demanded of us in *Rentenmarks*, we were unable to pay.

To the accompaniment of expletives from Helmut and his mother, we were forced with all speed to find somewhere else to live. The pale fiancée wept and slipped me a bar of chocolate as a parting gift. We stood in the street and good advice was almost as hard to come by as a new apartment.

Later, following an afternoon of failed attempts, we went to see Uncle Wally and Aunt Eva for a consultation. They too were extremely upset by Dr Schacht's clever move, but Uncle Wally had scraped together enough money over the past six months to enable them to hold out for a while at least. "Just sit tight," he advised. "Once the initial shock has passed, there will be business to be done here again."

"Not for me," my father said. "Tomorrow I'm leaving for Holland. I'll get a job there and Thea and Gittel must find cheap lodgings somewhere till I can have them come back."

Aunt Eva had already found rooms for us, in the house opposite theirs.

"Much more fun for Mili and Gittel," her affable voice consoled us. "It wasn't actually very nice at all for you to be living so far away."

She went with us to our new home and introduced us to the drab and melancholy Blumenfelds, who at once made clear that they found it dreadful to have to relinquish part of their spacious home to strangers. "It was different with Mr and Mrs Ray," the elderly woman complained. "They were friends. Mrs Ray was sunshine in the house and Mr Ray was such a true gentleman."

We were destined to hear a lot more about our predecessors. In every room, in a place of honour, stood a radiant photograph of the bright young couple. We were shown two sombre little rooms for which a surprisingly low rent was asked.

In the days that followed, my father left and Mili and I walked to school together again. On the way there every morning, from a first-floor window, we were honoured with blown kisses by a bespectacled man with a bald head and a goatee. We found it irresistibly funny and we sent his kisses back to him with exaggerated gestures. He seemed to like that a great deal, since he opened the window and threw us several dusty chocolate drops, which we accepted with an elaborate display of joy and gratitude. As soon as we were out of his sight we tossed them into the gutter, since Mili insisted it was a known fact that eating chocolates given to you by strange gentlemen could lead only to madness or death. Nanny walked with us a couple of times and on those occasions our bald friend hid behind the curtains like a coward.

My aversion to school was so powerful that I cannot call to mind either the building or the teachers and pupils.

At the Blumenfelds' I was not allowed to play the piano for more than an hour and a half each day. It was a strange instrument with a front made not of wood but of green silk, flounced and worn, which hardly improved the sound. The keyboard had lost most of its ivory and I scraped my fingers until they bled, but I did not give up the unequal battle, because Mrs Knieper had put the fear of God into me. That entire hour and a half on the Blumenfelds' piano was dedicated to her strict diet of arpeggios and scales: hard to endure but excellent for my musical health. Far worse was that at the end of every lesson, supposedly to encourage me, she had Hänschen come in and play. Green with envy I was forced to listen to his perfect rendition of *my* Mozart sonata and *my* "*Kinderszenen*" by Schumann.

Mrs Knieper never called the Netherlands anything but the countryside or the provinces, an intellectual desert completely devoid of performers of any importance. When I was audacious enough to nominate Mengelberg and Dirk Schäfer, she said with pride that both were Germans who had taken upon themselves the courageous and thankless task of introducing some sense of culture to a backward region, but that she had grave doubts as to whether they would succeed.

Her stories about Leona Frey made up for a lot. Her friendship with Leona was the glory and tragedy of Mrs Knieper's existence. She idolised the great *artiste* and at the same time was mortally jealous of her.

They had a birthplace in common, both later went on to attend the conservatorium, and they shared first prize in their final exams. After that, Mrs Knieper had done something very stupid indeed; she had fallen in love and married. Leona had been more sensible. She lived "à la carte" (I had no idea what was meant by that and did not dare to ask). And so it came about that Leona had reached the pinnacle of fame. She must, I reasoned, be a pleasant person, because every year, when she came to Berlin to play with the Philharmonic Orchestra, she stayed with the Kniepers, which surely would have represented a sacrifice for her. Moreover, she always gave a home concert for the friends and pupils of her old fellow student. The three best pupils were introduced to Leona and allowed to play for her, Mrs Knieper told me, adding, rather superfluously, that I was not among the chosen few. I would, however, be allowed to attend the recital, if I had not left for the provinces again by then.

I gave her my enthusiastic thanks for the invitation and assured her that it did not look as if we would be returning to the Netherlands for another six months.

9

MY FATHER'S LETTERS WERE NOT CHEERFUL AND THE end of our exile still seemed a long way off.

Mrs Knieper left with Hänschen for a ski resort that Leona was also to visit. If it was at all compatible with her concert tours, the pianist always spent Christmas and New Year with them.

The Blumenfelds told us that the previous year, a day before Christmas, Mr Ray had presented them with a twenty-pound turkey and on New Year's Eve the champagne had flowed like water. We could not match that. On 24th December my mother complained of a severe sore throat. She had a high fever. One floor above us lived a doctor and on Mrs Blumenfeld's advice I went to fetch him. He was the same age as the couple from whom we sublet. In reproachful tones he told her she was making a lot of fuss about such a "*kleiner Schnupfen*". Since I was on holiday from school I was free to play nurse. When I called in at Aunt Eva's for a moment to tell her my mother had a cold she immediately said, "Oh, then come over here this evening and enjoy a nice cosy Christmas with Mili. Uncle Wally and I are going to a party, so you'll have the whole place to yourselves with nanny. You can go and check on Mama every hour or so."

My mother got worse and worse. With closed eyes and a bright red face she kept calling out, almost unintelligibly, for ice. The Blumenfelds stayed well away and the doctor did not come back. Feeling as if I was committing theft, I took the last of the money out of my mother's purse. Somehow I had to get hold of ice. After much walking I bought half a block from a poulterer's. With my cold, hard, dripping load I got back home shivering and borrowed a hammer from the concierge.

My efforts were rewarded, since the crushed ice brought the patient a little relief. I still had a few marks left, so I went out in the afternoon to spend them as sensibly as I could. I bought a large bag of little chocolate meringues, which Mili and I had ogled every day on our way to school as we passed the window of a cake shop where they were stacked sky high in their brown, shiny glory. I would take half of them with me for Mili as my contribution to the Christmas cheer and my mother was certain to feast on the rest as soon as she was able to eat again. I could not resist the temptation to try one of the delicacies that I had looked at with such longing for weeks. It was a bitter disappointment. The meringue was burnt, all the little meringues were burnt, and five precious *Rentenmarks* were down the drain.

I spent the rest of the day nursing and in the evening I went to Mili empty-handed. Aunt Eva had laid out a magnificent buffet and we were invited to admire her in her dark-red, sparkling evening dress before she went out accompanied by Uncle Wally, who wore a midnight-blue dinner jacket.

To start off the festive evening we went with nanny to look at the Christmas trees on display in all the windows of the neighbourhood. There were some really beautiful ones and I said it was nice of the owners not to draw the curtains, so that Jews such as we, who did not have Christmas trees, could enjoy them too.

"Oh, Mama did want a Christmas tree," Mili said. "Mama joins in everything. If the Hottentots did something festive and she got to hear about it, she'd join in that too, she says."

One of the side streets we strolled along looked deceptively similar to a street I knew well. When I got to the end of it, in Antwerp, I would see Mr Mardell's house, cross over and ring the bell, and fat Bertha would open the door.

Right now I would not even mind receiving one of her slobbery kisses.

"No, but Gittel, what a surprise! How did you get here; how pleased Lucie will be. And how is your father doing?"

Yes, how was my poor father doing? He was no doubt sitting in a garret, starving, writing a letter to us by the flickering light of a stump of candle.

My mother ill, my father starving in a garret, and me, walking around in a strange city like a beggar. No, we were not doing well, but there was no need to tell good old Bertha that.

Menie, Salvinia and Gabriel would stick their heads through the office hatch. Although no, they would have gone home long ago by now, of course. Or might I have persuaded Gabriel to stay on for a while? Then later in the evening Lucie and I could walk with him along the River Scheldt by moonlight. Mr Mardell would open the honey door, ask if I wanted to look at his paintings, and say, "Tomorrow the October house will be hanging in its old place again". I would even be glad to see the lady with the green belly once more.

. . . and Lucie, my dear Lucie, how could I have forgotten about you for so long?

"Hello, little monkey," she would say. She called me that from time to time. "Hello my naughty monkey, why don't you ever write to me? Don't you see how ungrateful and disagreeable that is, when we have all been so kind to you?"

"I thought Gabriel was all you needed now."

"Nonsense."

Yes, that was it. I would write to her as soon as I had a postage stamp. Grandmother's house, where there was always a delicious smell of food, was not to be sneezed at either. I felt a dig in the ribs from nanny's bony elbow.

"What are you daydreaming about? We've already asked you three times whether we shouldn't go back home now and you act as if you're deaf. Where were you in that head of yours?"

"In Antwerp. I was thinking it will be very nice when I can go there again."

"Well," nanny said suddenly. "To tell you the truth I've had enough of Berlin too. I wish Papa and Mama would go back to Holland. Don't you, Mili?"

No, Mili liked it very much in Berlin, there were so many people, so many strange faces, and every face was a story.

"A sto-ry?" nanny asked, dumbfounded, and I did not understand either.

"Yes, every face is a story, and in most cases it's very different from the one the owners of those faces would tell you about themselves, but let's go home now, because after we've eaten all the lovely food we're going to let off some fireworks. Super," Mili said. Would she find it unpleasant, then, to go to Holland? Oh no, not at all, there were other people there too, with other faces.

I called in to see my patient, who was sound asleep, so I could devote myself to the festivities with a clear conscience. We first ate all the delicious things Mili's mother had left on display for us and then nanny brought out the fireworks. We were each given a dozen long, thin sticks, which we swung in the air after cautiously lighting them with a match. After a second or so they produced showers of purple stars that soon went out. The quicker you swung, the more stars. It was very exciting. At ten o'clock I said goodbye. Nanny, as ever, was profoundly happy to see me go. The concierge who normally guarded the entrance had been given the night off for Christmas. His place in the glass cage at the bottom of the stairs had been taken by a fat old woman who beckoned me over to her.

"You live across from here, with the Blumenfelds, right? And your mother is ill, right?"

"Yes, that's correct."

"What's wrong with her?"

"She has a sore throat," I said, amazed at the interest this completely unknown woman with her merry smile was taking in me.

"I thought so. The scoundrels. Your mother must have diphtheria. The previous tenant, Mrs Ray, who lived with the Blumenfelds, died of it. You didn't know that, right? Those rascals didn't tell you that, right?"

The fat lady shook with laughter.

"The doctor was part of the conspiracy, of course." She panted with delight, but when I started crying out loud it became clear that she was the sort who are born to pity, who are able to spare a bit of effort and helpfulness in exchange for the intense pleasure they take in the sorrows of their fellow creatures. I was to wait with her in the cage until her shift was over and then she would go with me to a different doctor, one who was not part of the Blumenfeld conspiracy. "And he will probably say your mother has diphtheria and then she'll have to go to hospital and what will happen to you then, poor child, all alone in a strange city?" She dug two packs of grubby playing cards out of her reed bag. To kill time she taught me "tens" and "the clock", and I taught her "sevens" and "pietje-peetje". The night concierge arrived at close to midnight. He was forced to listen to the whole story, as told in detail by the Samaritaness, and he expressed fulsome praise for her kind-heartedness. She rang a doctor who lived in the building, who she knew to be giving a Christmas party at home.

Ten minutes later a thin middle-aged man appeared in front of our cage in evening dress, furious at having been called away from his party.

Soon the three of us were standing at my mother's bedside. She was still sleeping. The doctor woke her and examined her with great thoroughness. The fever had subsided and the sore throat was less painful.

"Definitely not diphtheria," he decided, to the profound disappointment of my guardian angel.

"But the Blumenfelds must be told the real truth for once," she said. "You must do that, doctor."

"I most certainly won't. I'm going home."

The concierge believed she deserved a bit of fun after so much patience and charity. She went to the Blumenfelds' bedroom and I heard her yelling at the poor creatures for a full quarter of an hour.

She returned satisfied and made coffee. I gave her the meringues which, to my amazement, she ate with relish. When she had finally gone home, I tried to write to Lucie.

Beloved Lucie,

My sweet Lucie,

Dear Lucie,

I got no further than the salutation. How about writing to her father? I was always able to talk to him.

Dear Mr Mardell,

It's Christmas and I'm in Berlin and that's not as much fun as you might think . . .

The letter grew to four pages.

*

On 2nd January a message arrived from my father. He had found work and Grandmother had agreed to pay our return fare. Aside from a few bits and pieces, all our furniture had been sold and my mother envisioned us having to sleep on the floor for a year. Despite that prospect we were very glad to be leaving.

The Blumenfelds made no objection. The fools even let us go without demanding an extra month's rent.

Aunt Eva cooked a farewell dinner fit for a prince and confided in us that she too had had more than enough of Berlin.

"This time I'll be the one writing a letter to myself for a change," she said. "Saying we'll be home inside three months."

My hope of a visit to Antwerp soon after our return came to nothing. Grandmother, who as well as paying for our journey had been obliged to lend my father enough money to purchase the most essential items of furniture, was not prepared to welcome us there for the time being.

10

MR MARDELL ANSWERED MY CHRISTMAS LAMENT by express post, with a letter as solemn as it was affectionate. Lucie sent warm greetings along with it and I let them have our new address, to the extent that I knew it myself.

My father had rented a hideous furnished flat in Scheveningen, upstairs yet again. We lived hand to mouth as before, but after the Blumenfeld intermezzo it was paradise.

The first Sunday afternoon outing after our return was to the Mauritshuis, where I was received by the attendants like the Prodigal Son.

"Fine that she's here again, isn't it sir?" they each said in turn to my father, who had apparently sought comfort in the paintings and the friendly little old men.

The reunion with my music teacher went rather differently from the way I had imagined. I wanted to keep Knieper's devastating criticism from him, but he expressed a desire to hear all the new pieces I had been studying and so, stammering, blushing with embarrassment, I had to confess the shame of the scales. After I had played a few of them at his request, with the accompanying arpeggios, he growled that the witch had at least known what teaching was all about and out of the blue, with the unreasonableness typical of all adults, he was angry with me. He said that because I was his youngest pupil, he had been too lenient in his treatment of me up to now. That was over, and although he would be less strict than the Knieper woman, I should not expect him to allow me to start on Bach's "Italian Concerto" before I had made as much of the Beethoven rondo as that brat in Berlin had done.

Mili, accompanied by her parents and nanny, came back six weeks after us. They stayed with Grandpa Harry until they found a house they liked. Mili and I both went to a school in Scheveningen. This time she had more difficulty getting used to it than I did – she had lived longer in Berlin and liked it there – but after reciting her comfort verse every morning for a week on the way to school, she once again became the radiant centre of her class.

Grandmother said nothing, in all languages and none.

I had kept up my correspondence with Mr Mardell after my cry for help from Berlin. I still did not dare to write to Lucie herself, but from her father I heard that she was doing well. He quite often sent me programmes of concerts he had been to and sometimes he reported on them. We had been home for about six months when I received a highly authoritative review from him about a performance by violinist Jacques Thibaud. In a PS he wrote: *You will no doubt be pleased to hear that your granny and the faithful Rosalba are in the peak of good health. I assured myself of this yesterday. They in turn are very much looking forward to being able to welcome you to Antwerp soon.*

A day later we received a letter from my grandmother in which she invited us, with apparent sincerity, to come and stay with her, and oddly, when we arrived, she was genuinely pleased to see us.

Rosalba told me she wanted to help unpack our suitcases.

In the guest room she held my face between her hard hands.

"You know I'd have written to you if I'd have been able to," she whispered. At once I adopted the role assigned to me in Grandmother's theatre.

"Yes, of course, you didn't have time, you have so much work to do."

She shook her head. "You mustn't say silly things like that ... It's surely no scandal that I never had the chance to learn to read and write."

It certainly was a scandal, but no fault of hers. At that

moment I realised how much I loved Rosalba and I believe she knew it, too.

When my two young uncles returned from other activities – Fredie was studying law in Brussels and Charlie was "in diamonds" – they both expressed the belief that I had changed for the better. They thought the time ripe for them to make a contribution to my general development. A few days later Charlie brought me a wooden chest full of letters.

"Read these," he said. "And if you ever have the heart to write anything of the kind, I'll kill you."

The letters were from his countless rejected admirers. Charlie was small and ugly, but so conscious was he of his ability to enchant any woman he chose that he allowed his younger brother, who was far more handsome, to bribe him to absent himself whenever Fredie came home with a new flame. On the odd occasions when the tormented Fredie felt disinclined to accept such practices of extortion, he could be certain that the prospective catch would be snatched from him by Charlie with no trouble at all.

I was not interested in the letters from his victims and I told him that my father had taught me it was contemptible to read other people's correspondence.

"They're *my* letters now," he said. "And *I* say you must read them. Go on."

I read a few, albeit with reluctance.

"Well, what do you gather from that?" Charlie asked, in an intolerably priggish schoolmaster's tone.

"That they almost all end with: and now I'm going to take a bath and go to bed."

"Precisely," Charlie said. "And if you ever write such a thing to a man, I'm telling you now, I'll come and kill you, because it's the cheapest and stupidest kind of flirtatiousness there is. No young man worth tuppence would be snared by it. You don't really understand that yet, but just you remember it for later."

I growled that I had little need of advice for the future. I had been given it already by Uncle Wally.

"Really?" Charlie said eagerly. He was inquisitive by nature. "Do tell."

Uncle Wally had said, "When you're big, and married, you must never listen to courtship talk from other men. They always think: an established business is risk-free." He had added, looking contemplative, "Never forget: better a plate of pea soup properly served in the dining room than caviar gobbled down in the kitchen." When I asked him to explain these oracular utterances he refused, and Charlie, who grinned that this was all excellent advice, did not wish to pursue the matter either, so what was the point?

Fredie's contribution to my upbringing occupied a different sphere altogether and was far more pleasant. He was a bookworm and he urged me to read everything published in our language at the same time as he did. However, he also made me memorise long passages of prose and verse, which I then had to recite to his friends with what he regarded as the appropriate gestures and intonation. That was utter torment, since the young men wept tears of laughter at my absurd performance.

Whenever Fredie was in love he wrote verses himself, to which great value was attached, at least by the ladies for whom they were intended, and by him, and me. But it never lasted long, since his emotions were easily ignited and he had a new sweetheart more or less every week. For lack of time he became the creator of a useful off-the-peg poem. It went as follows:

> On my wall there is a clock,
> And every time it goes tick-tock
> It says to me, that little clock:
> Marie . . . Marie . . . Marie
>
> In the wood are many trees,
> They're tall, and old, and catch the breeze,
> What do they rustle, all those trees?
> Marie . . . Marie . . . Marie . . .

Then there were waves "washing over the sand" and birds, and a stream, and they all, each in its own way, gave a rendering of Marie . . . Marie . . . Marie, until a more attractive girl took possession of Fredie's inconstant heart for a while and then the whole lot murmured, rustled, tick-tocked and whispered a different name. He even lent the verse to friends whose eye had fallen upon young daughters with a feeling for poetry.

Mr Mardell had won my grandmother over to such an extent with his visit that she encouraged me to call on him soon, whereas in the past it had more or less annoyed her that I was so keen to be on the other side of the street. Bertha greeted me with a cry of joy and several damp kisses at the front door.

"How you've grown! How old are you now?"

"Thirteen, Miss Bertha."

She asked whether I was already a big girl. Yes, that was all in order now too.

Lucie came down the stairs. She looked pale and thin. She gave me a warm hug and put a silver chain around my neck from which hung a garnet in the shape of a heart. "To celebrate your safe return," she said. "Now first go and talk with my father, because he wants to hear all about your stay in Berlin. When you've told him everything, come upstairs and you'll get the traditional cup of hot chocolate." She kissed me again on both cheeks – she still had that wonderful smell of lily of the valley about her – and went back upstairs.

She was not the least bit interested in my experiences in Berlin.

Mr Mardell came out of his room and greeted me with a merry laugh and a cordial handshake. One of his pleasant qualities was that he neither gave nor expected kisses.

To my amazement I could "see" all his paintings. I asked whether he had bought new ones. No, he owned enough for the time being, right now he was more interested in masks and primitive sculptures. He showed me a few, which I thought ugly. "But your father says that I know what's beautiful before anyone else." We laughed together at that memory of my first visit. He wanted to hear all about the German mark and Dr Schacht and Knieper.

He said it was very good for me that I had faced my first negative criticism at such an early age, because negative criticism was always more instructive than positive criticism. For a start, it taught you who your real friends were. I told him of Mili's verdict on Hänschen. He asked whether she was that same sweet and clever friend of mine and said that one day, if I fulfilled my ambition and gave concerts, I would notice that certain people happen never to see the newspaper or magazine that has published a favourable review.

Mr Mardell had admired Leona at many concerts and even met her once, at a dinner with friends. No, she was not nice at all, but she was amusing and vain.

"Great artists are seldom lovable," Mr Mardell said, nor did they have any need to be. If they wrote good books, painted great paintings, or played as beautifully as Leona, they were already doing more than enough. There were far too many people in the world who could do nothing except be nice. I felt duty-bound to stick up for Leona; her friendship with the Kniepers over many years was clear evidence, was it not, that she must have a good character.

Mr Mardell did not agree. "Everyone needs a Theo," he said. "Mrs Knieper is Leona's Theo." Out of a cupboard he took a book with reproductions of paintings by Vincent van Gogh. He spoke at length about the painter's difficult life, which would have been unbearable but for the devotion of his brother Theo. "The success of almost every artist is built on the sacrifices of someone close to them. Only the very strongest can make their way alone."

I believe it was a helpful and interesting assertion, but I longed for Lucie. I was glad when Bertha came in with Mr Mardell's coffee. "Take her along with you," he said. "Since our friend is with us again for the first time, I'll drink coffee with the ladies and listen to find out if good musical progress has been made."

On the stairs he asked whether I had already said hello to Menie and Salvinia. He said I would be disappointed to hear that Gabriel was in London. Again my whole face coloured.

"Has he gone for good?"

"No, after six months he'll be back with us, I am happy to say. He so much wanted to go to England, and I was able to arrange it for him. He's working for a friend of mine."

Lucie hugged me again and Bertha put a cup of steaming chocolate in front of me.

"Everything is back the way it was," I said with a sigh of satisfaction.

At Mr Mardell's request I played my Mozart sonata. I was eager to hear his verdict. Technically I had made great progress, he said, and over time I would see for myself how Mozart's music changed. Now it was young and cheerful and later, much later he hoped, I would hear how melancholy and tragic it had become. Lucie protested: "What nonsense, Father. Tragic and melancholy. It's the most joyful music there is." Mr Mardell shook his head. "I'm pleased to hear that it's not yet clear to you that every note Mozart wrote sings that everything young must grow old and die and that all beauty is transient."

"Except for his own music, then," I managed to say.

"Except for the beauty of his own heavenly music," Mr Mardell conceded.

He drank his coffee and stood up. "I must go and get on with making a living." As he passed he stroked my hair. "Come and see us often, the way you used to, we're happy to have our friend here again, aren't we, Lucie?"

We heard him go downstairs and after he pulled shut the door to his room Lucie said, "Don't forget that you're still the only one who knows anything about Gabriel and me."

"So are you still engaged to Gabriel?"

I had been fervently hoping that she would meanwhile have realised her mistake.

"Yes, of course. Did you think it was over because he's gone to England? I'm glad he's there. But now you must do me a big favour," Lucie said, putting her arm around me. "You mustn't talk about Gabriel for the time being, because here the walls have ears."

I promised to be as silent as the grave.

I heard more about Gabriel than I wished to from Grandma Hofer. We now shared a guilty secret and her attitude to me had changed in every respect. Her friendliness even led her to assure me, time and again, "You don't need to be rich, you don't need to be beautiful. Luck is all you need!" Those encouraging words were followed by a long and confused story about some dirt-poor little monster or other who, against all expectations, in her old age, managed to scoop a reasonable fellow after all. My grandmother or one of the aunts would then immediately feel obliged to name several sweet beauties known to me who had somehow been "left on the shelf" because they did not have two cents to rub together.

My female relations, who had my best interests at heart, believed it could never be too soon to make me realise that I belonged among the pariahs, the outcasts of this earth – in our circles that meant girls who had no dowry. If such a destitute young woman remained unmarried, and if she came from a family regarded as distinguished, she must not try to earn a living in an office or a shop. She must pass her empty days in the parental home as her family's humble drudge, and they could make use of her unpaid services day and night, without uttering a word of thanks. If a girl married without a dowry she was perhaps worse off still. A woman who brought only herself and her love to a marriage counted for little. When the rosy mist of the honeymoon lifted she was no longer treated as an equal by her husband. If she had virtues and skills, they would be mocked and disparaged with relentless regularity by her in-laws, who would tease and pester her in every possible way until she was happy to give up the ghost. It was useful for me to know while still young what I was up against, and my female relatives, who showed courage in taking upon themselves the task of preparing me for a difficult future, were far from pleased by Grandma Hofer's fairytales, which they feared might undermine all the good work they had done on me – especially since they could not understand why we had become such good chums. After each of Grandma Hofer's visits they asked me to walk home with her and on the way she would tell me the latest news of Gabriel.

Since to my great annoyance I always turned bright red when his name was mentioned, she was of the opinion, just like Mr Mardell, that I was a bit in love with him.

Gabriel was doing very well in England. She hoped he would stay there for a while yet, although she missed him no end. "I'm glad he's away from those Mardells," she said. "They were a bad influence on him." Her son Jankel was the reason why Grandma Hofer visited Grandmother much more often now than before.

Uncle Jankel, Aron's father, had become estranged from us after the death of his oldest child. We did not see him often, and on the rare occasions when he came to a family gathering he spent the brief time he was with us wrapped in a distant, disdainful silence.

Jankel Hofer was a Midas; everything he touched turned to gold. As well as an important diamond business, he had shares in one of the major banks and now he and his family had moved to a veritable palace.

Despite the scorn of every branch of the family, he was

even toying with the idea of having himself appointed honorary consul to a Central American state and he had his beautiful house fitted out by the city's most famous interior designer. When it was finished we were all invited to come and view it.

Everything was very expensive and very new, and we came away deeply impressed. My father experienced a sad little triumph; of all the furniture and decorations that Jankel already owned, the only piece that had met with the approval of the interior dictator was a drawing my father had given his brother- and sister-in-law on the occasion of their marriage, showing Adam and Eve at the moment they were thrown out of Paradise. Since the subject did not appeal to the couple, Adam and Eve had always lived hidden away on the stairs to the attic, but after the move they were given a place of honour in my uncle's study.

As might have been expected, my uncle was keen to receive high-ranking guests in his distinguished environment. The family's espionage network operated without a hitch. We knew well in advance that Jankel was planning to give a grand reception for several leading figures of Antwerp and Brussels, and also that no-one in the family would be invited. This stirred up feelings to such an extent that Grandmother and Grandma Hofer declared a truce. At first they kept a stiff upper lip in each other's company, but that proved impossible to sustain and so, with wry satisfaction, they invented a new variation on the game "Qui Perd Gagne", bidding against each other with tall stories about the terrible ways they had been treated by their ungrateful offspring. Uncle Isi's many sins were discussed at length and to his mother his amorous excursions were not even the most unforgiveable part.

"Sonja knew what she was getting into when she married him," she said. "There are two sorts of men in the world, the boring and serious and the amusing and untrustworthy. The serious ones get to be sour as vinegar at an early age and the amusing are incapable of looking at a woman without pinching her bottom. I don't know which is worse. My husband was sour, whereas . . ." She blushed and swallowed the rest of her sentence. She had realised just in time that during a truce it was less than tactful to categorise my grandfather, of blessed memory, as one of the bottom-pinchers.

To my own amazement I was starting to appreciate Grandma Hofer and her adages. I even felt a degree of contrition at having in the past, when I was still living on the island, imagined her as the target of Blimbo's green stones.

She came to see us more and more often as the day of Jankel's party approached. The spy service had learned from the printer that the invitations were on hand-made paper with gilded edges, but none of the clan received one, although until the last moment everyone cherished an unspoken hope that Jankel would reconsider his inhuman attitude to his own flesh and blood and his relations by marriage.

On the morning of the fateful day my grandmother drank a cup of coffee with Grandma Hofer, my mother and me. She was in a state of acute grief. No mention was made of the party; the subject had become too distressing, and because we were incapable of talking about anything else we were sitting together in silence when Charlie came into the room singing and waving a package in triumph above his head.

"Have you ever heard of the silver leg, the silver leg of Jankel?" Charlie sang. Was he ill or had he gone crazy? Grandmother asked bitterly. If neither, then it was impossible to believe he had left his work in mid-morning purely to treat us to a rendition of the traditional song about maritime hero Piet Hein.*

Grandma Hofer confined herself to the mild observation that it might be a nice song if it was sung by someone with a good voice, but Charlie was delirious with excitement and impossible to calm. He danced around the room with his trophy and roared his incomprehensible version of the patriotic song until he ran out of breath. Then he sat down and said we must pay attention. He carefully opened the package and

* Piet Hein was a Dutch admiral and privateer, best known for the capture of a Spanish treasure fleet in 1628, a triumph celebrated in the words of the "Piet Hein song" that Charlie parodies here.

showed us the roasted leg of a giant bird, decorated with a frill ingeniously fashioned from silver paper.

Charlie was sent out every morning by his boss, who was blessed with a healthy appetite, to fetch filled rolls from Pelikaanstraat. In the shop's display case was a more than life-sized turkey, in full, solitary glory, with silver cuffs. It was those silver legs more than anything that had fired his imagination, Charlie said. He complimented Mrs Breine, the owner of the shop, on the grandiose creature, at which point the poor woman made the mistake of her life by saying he would see the bird again that evening at his brother-in-law's party, where the turkey was to form the impressive centre-piece to a procession of delicacies. She had been unable to resist the temptation to display her culinary masterpiece in the window. "That was her downfall," Charlie said. "Vanity must be punished." He had talked to her with such charm and for so long that in the end she cut off one of the legs; no woman could ever refuse him anything.

Rosalba came into the room and the four of us stared at Charlie, speechless with admiration. He said there was no point in giving him such hungry looks; he was not prepared to relinquish any of Jankel's leg. He had earned it fair and square all on his own and he was going to eat it himself. We expressed our wholehearted agreement and watched in awe as his strong young teeth made short work of the

190

substantial haunch. As a memento he put the silver cuff in his wallet.

Two minutes later a desperate Mrs Breine rang.

Jankel Hofer, who had come into the shop to give her a few pointers for the smooth running of his evening's festivities, had seen the mutilated turkey. Mrs Breine begged her enchanter to bring the leg back. She would be more than able to attach it to its rightful owner in such a way that no-one would notice, by means of some gelatine and mayonnaise embellishments, she claimed. Charlie told her in ghostly tones that the leg was deceased and went on to say he was surprised a respectable woman such as she could entertain such odd ideas. Just where on Mr Hofer was she intending to attach the leg? At that point Mrs Breine let fly at him with such ferocity that Charlie thought it advisable to settle the receiver gently back onto its hook.

Jankel's festive evening was passed in good cheer by his family. Led by Charlie we sang the song of the silver leg together and he was celebrated as the hero of the day. All the same, it was a pyrrhic victory.

Jankel never gave any of us the satisfaction of hearing a word from him about such an unimportant matter as a turkey. From time to time he did, however, nonchalantly tell a minor anecdote about this good minister or that pleasant governor before slapping himself on the forehead and saying in apologetic tones, "Oh yes, I'm sorry, I was forgetting you've never met him . . ." This would be followed by a quiver of indignation right across the board.

On the island my house was empty and Klembem no longer showed his face. On occasions I still heard his nasty little voice, but I knew that too would soon be gone. Another sign of approaching adulthood was that I had started to worry about my unattractive appearance. As soon as I found myself sitting in the quiet of his room with him again, I discussed the problem with Mr Mardell.

"You really aren't as ugly as all that," he said. "You look like your father and in general he is thought rather handsome, other than by your relatives across the street, who are so annoyingly proud of their straight noses. Actually, fanatical Zionists that they are, that nose ought to give them an uneasy sense of always flying under a false flag."

Afraid we were about to depart the subject that had taken hold of me, I voiced my anxiety that my strange face might perhaps obstruct me in my musical career. I could hardly conceal the broad jaws I had inherited from my father with a wavy beard, as he had done.

Myra Hess and Leona Frey were both so beautiful that it was as much of a pleasure to look at them as to listen. But in Mr Mardell's opinion, although this was no doubt a pleasant circumstance for both ladies, the true music lover did not care in the least whether an *artiste* was blessed with physical beauty. He named a large number of ugly geniuses of both sexes who sang, played, or danced to full houses all over the world. It was scant consolation.

Salvinia and Menie had been so frosty towards me on my first visit that I no longer dared to greet them. I told Bertha about it and asked whether she thought I might have insulted them in some way, by accident.

"They're not angry with you," Bertha said. "But they don't want to have anything to do with you because you get along so well with Gabriel. They're furious that he now has a higher position and a better salary than Menie. They think Mr Mardell gives him too much preferential treatment, this time with the trip and everything, and I believe they're right."

Deep down I thought Menie and Salvinia were right as well. Mr Mardell was far too good to that young man. He had even confided in me that he was planning to go and visit Gabriel at the end of his stay in England. As a reward for progress made, he intended to buy him a car and travel back with him in it, but I was not to say anything about that, as it needed to be a surprise. Because of Gabriel I was now keeping secrets for three people. It was starting to get on my nerves.

Our stay had been so amicable and peaceable for once that we even went home later than planned. We were accompanied to the train by all the women of the family plus

Rosalba and given enough food for a journey to Reykjavik. Grandmother stressed that we were invited to stay for a long time when we came back for her birthday.

The summer was less exciting than the summer of Bobby and Twill, and Grandmother's birthday was downright tame. This time Uncle Isi came to offer his birthday greetings as an exemplary father, thronged by his family, and everyone felt rather cheated. Grandma Hofer, who again asked me to walk a little way with her, told me that Gabriel was doing wonderfully well and that old Mardell had not seemed as bad as expected. In a few weeks from now he would leave for England and spend some time travelling there with Gabriel. I said I had known that for a long time, having heard it from the man himself, and Grandma Hofer asked whether I had been across the road yet. Since I could tell that even she was impressed by my friendship with the Mardells, it gave me great pleasure to be able to say offhandedly that I would be going to see them for the first time the next morning and after that I could go as often as I liked until we left for home.

My devotion to Lucie was well past its peak, but as soon as I was with her the old spell began working again so that, without thinking about it for a second, I became her accomplice when she asked me to.

On my first visit she announced that she wanted a serious talk with me.

"You're a very big girl now," she said. "I believe I can take you into my confidence, all the more so since you too are fond of Gabriel."

So, she thought that as well. I did not contradict her, although it was nonsense. She was silent for a long time. "Just you play something, then I can have a good quiet think." I was unable to play the piano while consumed with curiosity and Lucie said I could come and sit beside her.

"You know how much Gabriel and I love each other and that we would like to marry, but my father won't hear of it. Gabriel will soon be given a good job at an English bank. He has been brilliant at learning the language. He's doing very well, but my father is an obstinate, proud old man; even if Gabriel became director of the Bank of England, he still wouldn't allow me to marry him."

"How can that be? Your father loves Gabriel, he's so proud of him, he's going on a trip with him, isn't he?"

"There's nobody who can help me," Lucie said, sounding tragic. "Except for you. You've come back just in time."

"But Bertha is always keen to help you, isn't she?"

"I don't want that. When I'm gone there must be some-one left to take good care of Father. If he knew she had helped me elope, he'd throw her out the very same day."

"You're going to elope? Oh, how marvellous, just like in a book."

"Not marvellous at all," Lucie said sadly. "I'd far rather just marry from my parental home. Gabriel and I have had to wait all these years because now we no longer need my father's permission."

That was too complicated for me, but I blazed with fervour. "What do I have to do, Lucie?" Once again she thought for a long time. "First I have to write to my cousin, who lives in England, to ask if I can go and stay with her, because I need to be in the country for a fortnight before I can marry, and Gabriel and I want to do everything by the book. I'm not even going to stay in a hotel."

Again this was too difficult for me. Lucie went on, "Then, as soon as I know when I can visit her, I have to leave here one morning as if I'm just going out for the day, without a suitcase."

"Do I have to smuggle suitcases and clothes to you?"

"That would be very nice, but it's impossible. Where would you put suitcases in your grandmother's house? Everything would come out in no time. No, you must take my jewellery. There's not very much of it. The best thing would be to put it in your music bag. Nobody will look inside there and when I leave you can bring it to me at the station."

Lucie gave me a paper bag from a confectioner's. "Here's the first portion," she said. There was a pearl necklace inside with a diamond lock.

"Every day when you come to play I'll give you something."

I put the pearls between the virtuous, worn spines of Mozart and Brahms.

"When Gabriel made that bag for me he couldn't have imagined what it was going to be used for." Lucie smiled. "But I could," she said dreamily.

She wrote her letter to the English cousin that same morning. I had to smuggle that out too and post it. The cousin answered (poste restante) that Lucie was welcome to come and stay at any time and she decided to disappear the following Monday. She asked whether I thought I would still be in the city then and I was unable to say. In my hot-tempered family you were better off not making predictions.

Fate was on our side and on a sunny August morning, instead of going across the street as was generally assumed, I walked to the station, where I was to meet Lucie at the train bound for Calais. I was rather sad to be seeing her for the last time for a while, but it would be a relief to feel the jewellery was back in her safe keeping. She was wearing a light-blue summer dress. The train was not due to leave for another twenty minutes and I went to sit in the compartment with her. She thanked me for being such a great help and asked me to do her one last and difficult good turn.

"In a few days from now you must go to my father. He'll

always be willing to let you in, I'm sure. Tell him how distressing Gabriel and I find it that we had to take this step, but he left us with no other choice. I will write to him as soon as I'm in England, by the way, because I don't want him to worry about me. Tell Father that Gabriel and I love him very much and we hope that everything will soon be as good between us as it has always been." She kissed me and wished me success in my diplomatic mission. Then I had to get out of the train and I waved for as long as I still believed I could glimpse her happy face.

It was a difficult secret to keep, but my sense of responsibility silenced me. To my mother I said that I would not be going to Lucie's to play the piano because she was out of town for a short time.

After a few days I received a letter from London in which Lucie reminded me of my promise. Gabriel added a few lines and called me their brave fairy. I had yet to earn that honourable title. I imagined floating like a brave fairy into Mr Mardell's room and speaking such wise words to him that he shed a few tears of emotion and said, "Everything is forgiven and forgotten thanks to you, Gittel. Just write to my children and tell them they can come home straight away."

The following morning, cheerful and feeling assured of victory, I went to the house in which I had spent so many happy hours. I rang the bell and the door was opened by Bertha. She was startled at the sight of me. Tears rolled down her cheeks. "Oh, Gittel," she sobbed. "A great misfortune has befallen us." Salvinia stuck her head through the hatch. She was holding an index finger to her moustachioed upper lip. "Quietly now, quietly now," she hissed, with a nervous glance towards Mr Mardell's room. Bertha told me, still sobbing, that since receiving Lucie's letter Mr Mardell had refused to eat, sleep or speak to anyone; yes, that man known for his exquisite grooming had not even shaved, "as if he's in mourning".

Once again Salvinia warily stuck her head through the hatch. "He hasn't even spoken to us since the letter arrived," she whispered. "Menie and I are more or less carrying on by guesswork, we don't know what we're supposed to be doing, we don't dare go to see him and he hasn't rung for us yet." At that very moment he rang. Salvinia almost fell through the hatch in her eagerness to be with him as quickly as possible. "Thank God," Bertha groaned. "Now he'll get back to work as normal."

Salvinia returned straight away, white as chalk.

"He's heard that you're here," she said in an anxious voice. "And now he says you must go in to see him. Oh, aren't you scared?"

I felt if anything even more the "brave fairy" than before

and I shook my head in what I hoped was a brave and fairy-like manner. With Bertha and Salvinia staring after me in admiration I remained calm as I opened the gleaming blonde door. With a sweet smile I entered the familiar room. Mr Mardell was sitting at his desk, unshaven, emaciated and aged. When I closed the door behind me and walked towards him, still wearing that arrogant smile, he said:

"You . . ."

That single word was sufficient to make his profound distaste clear to me. My knees buckled and I could see nothing but the contemptuous look he was giving me. I went and sat in the chair facing him. He kept his eyes on me without saying anything.

"Mr Mardell," I stammered. "You mustn't be angry with Lucie or Gabriel, or with me."

"I see. I mustn't be angry," he said, his voice oddly strained. "I'll speak about Lucie and Gabriel in a minute, but first I have a bone to pick with you. Do you know what you are?"

All I was able to do was to shake my head.

"You're a traitor."

He stood up out of his chair and started pacing back and forth like an animal in a cage.

"A thankless traitor, that's what you are. I don't understand how anyone so young can be so craftily malicious."

"But Lucie and Gabriel love each other so much. He's such a wonderful young man, you said so yourself, and now you suddenly think he's not good enough for her."

"Not good enough? Not good enough? Who thinks that? He's selling himself to a much older woman, the fool. He'll regret it to his dying day, but I'll talk about my daughter and that idiot in a moment. Right now I'm talking about you, traitor. Aren't you ashamed?"

He had always been good to me. He had hung that precious painting above the piano to give me pleasure. He had listened with patience when I asked for advice or an opinion and it was awful to see him unshaven and crumpled, no longer the worldly, elegant Mr Mardell, only a sorrowful, hurt, angry old Jew. I started crying.

"You must think you've played a great role in this sad story," he went on. "Nothing could be further from the truth. That pair would have got away perfectly well without being aided and abetted by you. God knows, my daughter is of age. Thirty, she is, the madwoman. In England she didn't need my permission, but until she was thirty she couldn't touch her mother's legacy. Still, we're not talking about that now, we're talking about you."

He had circled the room again. The whites of his eyes had turned yellow and one eye was bloodshot. He let out a loud laugh. Bertha and Salvinia, who had been pressing their ears to the door in an effort to follow everything that was said, ventured to come in when they heard him.

"At least you're laughing again," Bertha said, relieved. "I'll go and fetch your breakfast."

"Away with you," snarled Mr Mardell. "I'm not done with this young lady yet." And when she hesitated he picked up a book and made as if to fling it at her head. They both shot out of the room and that terrible laughter began again. "You're such a stupid child, eh? Such a complete fool, and those two clever creatures were well aware of that. They knew I was very fond of you, and indeed I was." He looked at me. "You knew that too, didn't you? If you hadn't helped those two, you could have taken Lucie's place, but that cunning pair neatly put a spoke in the wheel by getting you involved in their elopement. They know I can forgive anything except treachery and ingratitude." He walked around the room one more time until he was standing next to my chair. "I never want to see you again."

I stood up to leave.

"Sit down. I haven't finished yet. The least you can do after behaving so splendidly is to listen to me in silence and not snivel and look at me when I'm speaking to you. In a minute or two I'll throw you out of the door and don't you dare let me lay eyes on you ever again, but before you leave here for good, I'm going to make a prediction. You'll be unhappy all your life long and always make the wrong moves. Everyone you trust will betray that trust. And when people mean well by you, you'll be too stupid to appreciate that for what it's worth. I may very well restore my daughter and that clever character, my son-in-law, to favour after a while, but I'll never forgive you. My son-in-law! How killingly funny!"

He came to stand next to me. "No doubt you think Gabriel is truly in love with my daughter. Not at all. Have you read *Camera Obscura*?"*

"Yes, Mr Mardell."

"Then you know about Keesje, who wanted to improve his corpse. That's what Gabriel wanted as well and he thought this was the best way to be certain. For you there is no certainty. You're like your father, except that he realises he's a *schlemiel*. You'll always believe you have happiness within reach and you'll never encounter anything but disappointment and sorrow." All at once I remembered Mrs Knieper's cups full of sorrow and joy, and stammered that at least I would be able to learn to play the "*Appassionata*" properly. Mr Mardell was silent for a moment and then he cursed me.

* *Camera Obscura* is a collection of short pieces by Hildebrand (Nicolaas Beets, 1814–1903) that was hugely popular in the nineteenth century and beyond. The character Keesje is a poverty-stricken old man desperate to ensure he will be able to pay for a proper burial and buy his own shroud.

203

"Perhaps you will indeed learn that one day, when you're very old." He laughed. "But then there will be no-one who wants to listen to you. Or did you honestly think you could become a famous concert pianist without having money, power or intelligence?"

I stood up and felt my way to the door. In the hallway I bumped into Salvinia and Bertha, who began interrogating me. Mr Mardell opened the door. He looked like his old self again.

"Come back for a moment, Gittel. There's something else I need to say to you. I'm no longer angry." I didn't dare go back into the room and I crept away behind the two dismayed women. "You may write to Lucie to tell her that in a few months from now she can come and visit me. You'd enjoy doing that, wouldn't you? Now give me your hand, then at least we'll part good friends. But don't be disappointed if you never hear anything from Lucie or her husband ever again. See it as a lesson in life."

"Go on," Bertha coaxed. "Give Mr Mardell your hand." But I was no longer able to. I ran outside in search of a place to recover.

At the start of the avenue every bench along the central path under the trees was occupied by mothers with wailing children. Further along I at last found one where a grimy old woman was curled up fast asleep. There was just enough space left to sit crying next to her without bumping her worn-out shoes.

Craftily malicious, Mr Mardell had called me, and so I was; a complete idiot, that was true too. But why was he so furious that Lucie wanted to marry Gabriel if the young man was far too good for her, as he had said?

My fruitless contemplation was disturbed by a clear voice. "No, but if that isn't Gittel! What's wrong? Have you hurt yourself?"

Dazed, I looked up at a tall, blonde young woman carrying a heavy bag of fruit and vegetables in either hand. Leeks, parsley, cabbage, apples and melons stood out cheerily against the cornflower blue of her cotton dress.

"Don't you recognise Odette Bommens any longer?"

She had changed almost beyond recognition; far slimmer and more energetic, she seemed ten years younger than when I last saw her.

She looked at me with concern. "What's happened to you and how do you come to be sitting next to that old vagabond?" She had broken herself of the habit of sighing at the start of every sentence.

I preferred not to talk about my misery.

"No need, either," Madame Odette said. She quite understood. But now that I was so close by I must go with her for a moment to say hello to Arnold. They were all fine. Robert and

Lucien were happy at school and she was very much enjoying working with her brother.

After the glare of the sunshine in the streets, my burning eyes could at first make out little in the velvety half-light of Arnold's bar. Once I had adjusted to it, I admired the old furniture, the gleaming copper, and the bar itself, which was ornamented with gilded foliage like the proudest of barrel organs.

Odette said a glass of beer would revive me. She tapped it expertly, with a firm head, without spilling a drop.

Then she asked me to polish up a carved Mechelen dresser that she had waxed. Meanwhile she would make coffee.

I was allowed to devote myself to the most difficult corner, where three gentlemen in mediaeval costumes with raised goblets waved at passers-by. First I removed excess wax from the grooves with a split matchstick and then it was a matter of vigorous polishing.

"There's no better cure for women's sorrow than polishing wood or brass," Madame Odette said. She had often yearned to do it while the baroness was alive but had been forbidden to take any work away from the staff. "It was a great disappointment to Mama that I remained such an ordinary girl, whereas she was a real woman of the world."

Arnold Bommens was summoned from the wine cellar and he hugged me in his own warm-hearted way.

I allowed myself only a few minutes to relax and drink Odette's excellent coffee. Two of the Mechelen gentlemen were gleaming, goblets and all, and it was a matter of pride to me not to leave the third dull. When Arnold asked whether I felt like some waffles, his sister said that he ought to know I was not allowed to eat them on account of my religion. Craftily malicious as I was, I lied that waffles were permitted. After an hour, Madame Odette took me home, but she refused to go in with me. She no longer visited real ladies. I thanked her for the pleasant morning and she said in parting that I must promise her never again to cry over a man, because none of them were worth it.

My ordeals were not yet over. At home I could hear even from the stairs the loud, monotone voice of the girl to whom Charlie was to become engaged in a few weeks. Like all new aunts she felt obliged to be affectionate in the extreme towards her freshly acquired nephews and nieces. She therefore greeted me with a cry of joy and a wet kiss. Charlie's choice was a mystery to me at the time. His future wife was inelegant and tiresome. The sound of her voice, moreover, invariably gave me a splitting headache. Since then I have learned that men who succeed in luring delightful women away from other men think that the unattractiveness of their own lawful spouses will safeguard them against the horns they were so happy to plant on so many heads in their wild years.

"Have you been playing some nice piano at the Mardells'?" the unpleasant voice of my newest aunt shrilled, and I was just trying to think of an appropriate answer when the door to the room was flung open by Grandma Hofer.

Without looking to left or right, without greeting anyone, she came straight towards me. Standing in front of me, she carefully removed her black kid gloves. She laid them on the table. "You knew," she said. "Devious brat." And she slapped me on each cheek in turn, which made me see stars. Grandmother, Rosalba and the young aunt, who had watched the assault frozen with shock, all started protesting in unison, but Grandma Hofer calmly pulled on her gloves again.

"Did you deserve that or not?" she asked.

I said I had deserved it, since otherwise she could not have left the house unmolested by the three furious women.

"What in God's name have you got on your conscience?" Grandmother asked.

Without saying anything I raced up the stairs to the guest room.

That afternoon Charlie took the news of Lucie's elopement to the diamond exchange with him. I heard a great deal about my skulduggery, but none of them ever came to know how closely involved I had been in the affair. Mr Mardell must have sworn Salvinia and Bertha to silence by some ruthless means.

To Lucie I wrote a short letter in which I told her in a businesslike tone that she would be able to visit her father after a few months had passed.

One of his predictions came true straight away. She did not reply.

II

ROSALBA'S DEATH WAS AS QUIET AND MYSTERIOUS as her life. Fredie found her one morning, lying unconscious at the bottom of the stairs. She was clasping the tray on which she had been taking Grandmother's breakfast upstairs so firmly in her calloused hands that it was a struggle to free it from them.

She lived for another few days, unconscious for the most part. Grandmother refused to allow her to be taken to a hospital and would not hear of fetching a nurse. For thirty-seven years Rosalba had been her faithful companion, she said, and no strange hands would be allowed to care for her now.

She thought she was doing the right thing by calling an Anglican priest to the bedside, since with the end in sight Rosalba might perhaps take some comfort in the faith she had neglected during her life. The elderly clergyman had just taken up his place next to the dying woman and was murmuring a prayer when she looked up and saw him standing beside her bed.

Her eyes sought my grandmother's. "What's this old *goy* doing here?" she asked. "Send him away, I don't need him."

They were the last words she ever spoke.

Rosalba had always been a modest little figure in the background, but Grandmother's house was silent and empty without her when we returned there after the funeral.

The priest attended the burial with us and he was able to deliver a long and moving speech beside Rosalba's open grave now that she was unable to protest at his presence. After several weeks of deep mourning, Grandmother found a young, cheerful Jewish girl from Brabant willing and able to take over Rosalba's duties. Her joyful presence transformed the atmosphere in the house. All the uncles, married or not, fell in love with her at first sight and it was entertaining to see how skilful she was at warding off their advances with a joke.

Grandmother entered her second childhood. She bought several pearl-grey and lavender-coloured gowns that were not the least bit reminiscent of Queen Victoria. She travelled a great deal and gambling fever took hold of her. In Ostend and Spa she was a welcome guest at the gaming tables. Grandma Hofer, who had her spies everywhere, knew to the last franc how much Grandmother was gambling away and informed her disconcerted offspring.

After a few months, at a family meeting convened in haste, the possibility of placing her under legal restraint was raised, but after much discussion the assembly dispersed without having come to a decision.

Grandmother put an end to her brief period of intoxication with freedom by having a stroke, which made it impossible for her ever again to escape the tender vigilance of her children.

When I saw her for the last time she looked decades older.

The coquettish wig that had caused such a scandal had become far too heavy for her. Across her lopsided face, the left half of which was paralysed, hung a few thin wisps of white hair. Only with difficulty could she say a few words, most of them incomprehensible.

Once, when I was sitting alone at her bedside, she said, quite distinctly, "I'm glad I won't see the horse chestnuts blossom next spring."

She struggled to tell me how she had buried her first child somewhere in a far-off land. She could no longer remember where it had been, "But he was such a beautiful little boy." She cried in that heart-rending way old and sick people have: loud sobs without tears. "And all the horse chestnut trees we passed on the way home, so many chestnut trees, full of white and red candles . . . I always hated them after that."

She was my grandmother yet I felt as if I was sitting next to a stranger. Mili said that every human face contains a hidden story, but only wise eyes could read it properly.

Just how lonely and bitter my grandmother's life had been, despite her large family, became clear after her death from the final lines of her will, a copy of which was made for each of the women in the family.

"My urgent advice to my daughters and granddaughters is as follows: never retain staff for more than five years at the most."

So I had misread Rosalba's secret story, too.

The last time I went to stay with my grandmother I noticed that the Mardells' house was unoccupied and notices from an estate agent were stuck up outside.

Lucie had stayed on in London with Gabriel, while her father, awaiting an immigration visa for the United States, was living at a hotel in Brussels.

Gabriel never saw his beloved Antwerp again. He died suddenly a few years later of a lung disease.

Within six months, after the usual rigmarole that the sharing out of an inheritance brings with it, my mother received her portion. The sum was larger than expected.

Once all our debts had been paid off, there was enough left to buy a house and even a small amount to invest in a suitable business venture. My father would have liked to move us all to Mesopotamia, the land of his dreams, without delay. Why he felt so attracted to the place never became clear to me. Its resonant name probably aroused thousand-and-one-nights associations in him. Uncle Wally had to be called in to dissuade him from the wild adventure, and as a token of gratitude he, Aunt Eva and Mili were invited to dinner to celebrate our restored prosperity. During dessert Wally stood up and tapped his wine glass. He asked us to join him in drinking to a man who, although all the virtues were united in his person, was not quite valued at his true worth by his contemporaries, or even by those closest to him who had the privilege of enjoying his outstanding qualities daily. "An excellent husband, a devoted father, a true friend." Uncle Wally had to stop for a moment to recover himself, while my father smiled with gratification and modestly cast his eyes downwards. "A man," Wally went on, raising his voice, "who does not allow himself to be struck down by adversity but who, when appropriate, knows what it means to celebrate. A man, to put it succinctly, such as is born no more than once in a hundred years. I invite you, esteemed fellow diners, to drink a glass to the health of our own Wally!"

When we had recovered from the indignation this

produced we took turns giving speeches in praise of our own outstanding qualities – apart from Aunt Eva, who got no further than "Esteemed fellow diners" before succumbing to the giggles.

After dinner, geniality personified, she offered her help in furnishing our new house. She pulled me onto her lap and wrapped her arms around me. "What colours do you want for your bedroom, Gittel?"

"Oh, blue or something," I said, unconcerned. My mother complained that I had been so disgruntled of late that there was no reasoning with me, but Aunt Eva always had a justification to hand.

"You'll see how nice she'll find it once we get going," she said. "You mustn't forget that she's been through an awful lot over the past year. She's still sad about her grandmother and Rosalba, of course."

During the previous year I had been through far more than she imagined and I wanted to be circumspect and cautious, like the wise virgins. I had no intention of mourning for two women who hated each other. Rosalba had been a sly tease and the true reason for Grandmother's faithful vigil at her bedside – a profound joy evoked by the death throes of her tormentor – was horrifying. I no longer wanted to think about the Mardells and Gabriel, nor could I allow myself to be happy at the improvement in our financial circumstances, because my father's way of doing business meant it was quite likely to be of short duration. I would jolly well watch out and not fall for anything anymore, which meant I would never be able to play the "*Appassionata*" well, and meanwhile I was still sitting on Aunt Eva's lap and I could not make her wait any longer for an answer.

"You've guessed right," I whispered in her ear. "I'm still sad about Grandmother and Rosalba." And as I was saying it, I realised with gratitude that it was not a lie.

Scheveningen, 1958

A SHORT GLOSSARY

Beschwipst – [German] tipsy

goy/ pl. *goyim* – [from Hebrew] a non-Jew/ non-Jews

kugel – a kind of pudding served as a main course or as a side-dish

lehavdil – [Yiddish] to make a distinction (between two very different things)

mauvais garnement – [French] villain, rogue, scoundrel

meshuga – [from Yiddish] mad, crazy, stupid

rabbanim – [Yiddish] plural of rabbi

rebbetzin – [Yiddish] wife of a rabbi

Schieber – [German] black marketeer

schlemiel – [from Yiddish] an awkward or unlucky person

Schmiere – [German] fleapit

Shabbat – [from Hebrew] Sabbath

shamus – [Yiddish] sexton of a synagogue

sheitel – [from Hebrew] wig worn by a married Jewish woman

shnorrer – [Yiddish] beggar, sponger

shul – [Yiddish] synagogue

unter den Linden – [German] under the lime trees. Also the name of the boulevard in central Berlin to which the passage refers

yeshiva – [Yiddish] An Orthodox Jewish college or seminary; a Talmudic academy

IDA SIMONS (Antwerp, 1911 – The Hague, 1960) came to the Netherlands with her parents during the First World War. At the age of nineteen she made her debut as a pianist with the Cercle Musical Juif in Antwerp. Her star quickly rose after her musical studies in London and Paris, and she performed with many major orchestras at home and abroad. Her career was cut short by the German invasion of the Netherlands. After the war she performed again and even toured the United States, but she had to abandon her musical career and instead began to write. She made her debut in 1946 with the poetry collection *Bitter Harvest*. In 1959 she published her much-praised novel *A Foolish Virgin*, which also appeared at the time in German translation. Since its republication in 2014 it has been translated into twenty-two languages.

LIZ WATERS is the translator of fiction by Lieve Joris and Annelies Verbeke, and of non-fiction by Douwe Draaisma, Geert Mak, Linda Polman and Louise O. Fresco, among others.